THE BOTTOM OF ANOTHER TALE

The Bottom of another Tale is a rare blend of legends and maxims. Free flowing contemporary African tales suffused with native wisdom and riddles. The collection is quite a delight. Engaging, the tales are short, crisp and pregnant, with diverse messages.

- Tubal Rabbi Cain, multiple award winning poet and author, *Mystery in our stream* and *Dandaula and other African Tales*.

Dense thoughts, dense happenings, linkages and intertextuality; a writer's attempt to tread the thin line between dreams and reality, *The Bottom of another Tale* is a daring attempt, an ingenious departure from the norm.

- Maria Ajima, literary scholar and award winning author of *The Survivors* and *Cycles*.

Agema's stories are peopled by unforgiven men, gods and demons. They are delivered with a candour that reminds us of the brutality of reality and the arbitrariness of existence, bringing to fore Agema's keen sense of observation as an emergent voice on Nigeria's literary landscape.

- Abubakar Adam Ibrahim, Caine Prize 2013 Shortlist, award winning author of *The Whispering Trees*.

These stories glow like burnished nuggets of gold. Su'eddie has a mastery of words and a gift for story telling that is uncanny in its uniqueness and inspiring in its application. To read his words is to escape to a world of verisimilitude, where culture, politics and societal nuances are revealed with subtle wisdom, endearing warmth and light spirited humour, not only as they are but as they should be. These stories are as thoroughly entertaining as they are viscerally enlightening.

- Jude Idada, award winning playwright and author of *Oduduwa: King of the Edos*.

The short story can take whatever length but what it must do is occupy a much larger space in the mind. This is precisely what Su'eddie does... I have been ruminating over these stories: I have been chewing them over and over in the manner of the goat chewing the curd.

- Hyginus Ekwuazi, multiple award winning poet, author of *Love Apart* and *Dawn into moonlight: all around me dawning*.

Su'eddie paints pictures with words and leaves us with refreshing, unforgettable tales. This collection is lovely!
-	Pever X, author, *Cat Eyes*

In these stories, Su'eddie is able to balance very perceptive prose with serious and contemporary social concerns. An impressive debut.
-	Richard Ali, literary critic, editor and author, *City of Memories*.

~ THE BOTTOM ~
OF ANOTHER TALE

(SHORT STORIES)

Su'eddie Vershima Agema

SEVHAGE
PUBLISHERS
CONTEMPORARY AFRICAN SERIES 9

ISBN: 978-978-525-95-6-8

SEVHAGE

An Imprint of VERSHAGE Enterprises

Black Gate Trove, No 3, MFM Street, Karu, Nasarawa State

Administration and Correspondence:

S 23, Top Floor, No 62 Old Oturkpo Road,

P. O. Box 2192,

Makurdi, Benue State, NIGERIA.

www.sevhage.com

http://sevhage.wordpress.com
http://vershage.wordpress.com

sevhage@gmail.com

Makurdi. Karu. Abuja. Ibadan.

P.O. Box 2192, Makurdi, Benue State

+234 (0) 807 358 0365; +234 (0) 809 248 7423

Cover Picture and Design: Eugene Odogwu

Earlier versions of some of the stories in this collection have appeared in the Blueprint Newspaper, Nigerian Pilot Newspaper, online at YNaija, Naijastories (http://naijastories.com/author/sueddie), Sentinel Nigeria E-zine, http://sueddie.wordpress.com, http://loladeville.com, among others. The Publisher is grateful to every one of them (and even those omitted) for the opportunity.

~ DETALES ~

A Final Short Story...

For Mbatsavde Emmanuel, Chris Ayede-Agema, Pat Iorpuu & T. V.
Agema
who taught me much

Also for

My siblings; *Tavershima, Gabriel, Sever, Theodora & Ver*

Sabastine Niagwan & Tardoo Ayua

Who participated in the early rites.

THE RIVER'S TESTAMENT

On this night, it wasn't the buttocks of the calabash that hung above. It was the half, in the words of the people. Tombo chuckled to himself. The buttocks referred to the full moon while the half was its half. The villagers claimed the moon showed the various positions of the Almighty drinking from the vastness of the skies. Whatever that meant—*crap!*

He was not the sort of African who believed in such nonsense. Traditions were old pieces of caution and actions that had been created for specific events. Ignorant people continued them even when the importance had long faded. It was like the tale of the lady who fried sausages by cutting the two edges off because "her mother did so," as she always told anyone who cared to ask. When asked why she did so in her day, her mother simply replied, "I never had a big pan so I had to chop the edges so the sausages would fit into the small pan I had!" He couldn't remember where he had read the story from, but it sure fit the situation. It was all about civilization, and nothing more. Technology and the new age sure hadn't done much to many locals and Bantaje was a testimony.

After his graduation, Tombo had been posted to Bantaje to *compulsorily* serve his nation for a year as a Corps member. He was one out of twenty others who had been sent to the village to assist in a government scheme aimed at uniting people of all tribes in the country. He was a teacher at the local community school there. He taught English Language and Literature to students, most of whom couldn't communicate in English. Tombo always thought his task gargantuan till he walked in on Lateef, a fellow Corps member trying to teach Accounts and Mathematics! The frustration that adorned Lateef's face was enough to make Tombo count his blessings. He might have smiled and managed it all but the job grew more stressful with additional classes assigned to him. The trick had been to make him sign an agreement to teach the SSS 1, 2 and 3 classes. He had no idea that each of the classes had five arms each, A-E!

Besides work, there were other challenges—those of life in general. When the Corps members had arrived in Bantaje at first, they were told that drinking water was sourced from the community river or a close-by well. They resolved to drink only bottled water bought from a nearby town. Soon, issues of economy forced them to downsize to satchet water. It wasn't long before they decided to use water from the well. When the dry season came, a new wisdom directed their feet to the river to fetch their water. But that wasn't all. Most of the young ladies in Bantaje were not always allowed to come out in public and usually stayed indoors. The only exception for most was school, their washing day, and the night of the full moon. So, though Tombo had spotted a lady—he would later find out to be Rekia—he could not experiment some of the scenes he was crafting for a text in his head. He scribbled several poems to this elusive love of his but each day increased his unease and longing. How could one survive like this?

He exchanged the hell he found for a bit of bliss provided in the opportunity to learn more of the language and traditions of the people—more for literary material to aid his writing than for acculturation. He discovered another side to Bantaje too.

Now, Bantaje was, and is, a peaceful village with good people. It had a beautiful landscape and a river too—a writer's delight. Tombo found relief in these and somehow, began to enjoy himself a bit. That was till the superstitions began to pour in. They started at first, humorous, ridiculous, and the like:

"Strike a left foot; bad luck. Strike a right foot; good luck." If one happened to break one's right leg while faking this, it was the person's misfortune for luck smiled—or frowned—only when it happened accidentally. There was no cheating the gods. There was; "If you hear an owl hooting; ill omen." For their information, in certain parts of South Africa where he had spent his formative years—and the lands of better thinking people—owls were good omens bringing better fortunes and wealth. This was the one that gave a big question mark to the universality of the gods. Sure, this was where they would deny it and say that the different lands had their gods. Nevertheless, they emphasized the owl omens more and advised him not to go to the river then. An eerie one was that of the stars; "the amount of stars you see on a specific night are the amount of days you have remaining over here." In essence, if you were unfortunate to look into the skies on a starless night, the next day would be your death!

"Don't go out on the night of the half moon, it is the time of the preparation. This is the time between the fullness and starvation." This was the tricky one. One could never be sure of which side one's luck would roll. It was best to be careful rather than test the favour of the gods, or so the people said. Tombo once wondered aloud if the gods could be bribed to get favours. The emphatic answer, accompanied with looks of disgust, was an emphatic "No!"

But even in the midst of most of the don'ts, there was a night of bliss to look forward to; the night of the full moon. All could go out and play about; children and adults. It was the time when nature was fulfilled. It was the reason for the illumination, the clear essence that was always visible on such nights. This was why most societies had their dances and other such beautiful rituals on this particular night. This was one of the few myths he had loved.

On the last full moon, Bantaje had come out in splendour. The stars had sparkled the night to accompany the big ball of the sky. An old man told stories to children in the middle of the village. He had scared the children with tales and passed on more of the usual myths and superstitions. Tombo had stayed by for a while and laughed. *Yes, this was more like it*, he thought to himself. He understood the myths in the spirit of the tales told only. There were initiation rites in some corners and the more attention grabbing sensation—a good number of ladies swinging hips that had left Tombo inspired for over a week. But more than that, he had used the opportunity to corner his muse, Rekia. The moon seemed to shine in her face. He was enraptured. She told him that she was only allowed to come out on the night of the full moon.

"Why don't you come on the half moon too?" Tombo had asked with a mischievous wink.

She giggled lightly; "Maybe I would one day, but you know about the half moon, *abi*?"

"Who knows, the next one could be the one on which we would have fun."

"You are really funny."

"For you, *true talk*, I could be funnier..."

"You don't believe in our traditions?" Rekia challenged.

"Not at all. I think they make for good humour, great laughter and all but that is it..."

"What about the one of the river?"

"The river? I haven't heard about it. Tell me. Everyone that goes into it on a Friday night would turn into a dashing wealthy man?"

"No! The river has the power to kill."

"Oh please! Spare me!" Tombo had returned in jest. Till that point, he thought he had heard the most ridiculous of the myths. He had laughed out loud but Rekia was serious.

"True! It has the power to kill o!"

He laughed louder this time.

"I will tell you what has powers to kill."

"What?"

"My own new superstition..."

"Yes?"

"You, Rekia. You have the power to kill every defence of mine."

She smiled. The flow continued and it wasn't long before he found her in his arms, and boy, was it a hug! He pushed for a kiss but the lady didn't think that one night was enough to grant such favours.

"But it is the night of the fullness!" he protested.

"I thought you didn't believe in any of the myths."

"Well..."

"Maybe you would wait a few more moons to see if you are worthy..."

She blew him a kiss which he caught to his chest. It was time to go and far before he would have wanted, the night was out. He decided Rekia was worth several moons.

Oh yes, he could believe in the full moon forever if it came like that! *But for all the other superstitions, myths and traditions, they are funny but obsolete, and need redefinition,* Tombo thought. Well, all but the mysterious one of the river that Rekia had mentioned. It seemed she had told everyone else to sing it into his ears.

"The river has power to kill, directly or indirectly." One of the elders said for maybe the one millionth time. They kept throwing it at him because of his deep love for the river. He always found inspiration to write when he went there. Now, he didn't really mind at first but as with the things that are always pushed into one's face, he got tired of it one day. Tombo had had enough.

"Baba, I am sorry but no, it doesn't."

"It does..."

"Okay, I will try it one of these days." Tombo challenged.

"Aj! No! Please, don't. We have a saying here on advice taken and ignored: *Don't do* or how do you put it in English? *Aha!* Don't do—thou *shall not—is* medicine; ignoring *don't do* is death. So, *don't do* is the medicine, the committing is the death. Life is preserved in the opening of one's ears to wisdom..."

"Baba, you don't need to say anything more. It doesn't work."

He spoke to a few more people who assured him that the river had the power to kill. He waited for the night of the half. Noting the proper day of the half, he selected the clothes for his small adventure. Satisfied, he fell into a deep slumber in preparation for the night.

*

He laughed again at the half of the buttocks of the calabash. He looked at the stars and noted that there was none in the sky. Did that mean he was going to die tonight or tomorrow? He smiled. He stuck his earpiece into his ears, put his ink to his writing pad, and let the verse flow. After a while, he decided to take a quick dip in the river. The words of one of the other people he had spoken to came back to his ears:

"The river has a life of its own. It is a force that kills."

"How? Very funny."

He smiled again as he pulled down his boxer shorts. He removed the earpiece and the sound of the howling winds came to his ears: *Pheeeeewwwww! Pheeeeeeeew!* He shivered and looked around. There was no one about. He had second thoughts. Was that the sound of an owl in the distance? He closed his eyes and ran to the banks. He jumped into the river as it splashed. He expected a fish to bite at his middle as he landed but it was just the water that *jumped* out. He swam a while with fear playing bass drums in his heart. There was that little thing somewhere that kept tugging at his soul. Minutes of no danger soon reduced the drums to a tom-tom and rekindled a bit of his old self assurance. Soon, his stomach started singing. He knew the bushes were calling so he came out of the water. The bushes were a little distance and there were chances that someone would come by. He considered this and put his boxer shorts on. He answered the call. The words, 'force of the river' came to his mind again. Could it be that the river would influence a snake or some wild thing to come and bite him? He imagined a snake coming to bite his buttocks. There was a sound in the bush. He jumped up and pulled up his boxer shorts. He ran a few paces, only to discover that the 'scarer' was a frog. He hissed and bent down at his new location to continue his business.

* *

Like other days, he woke up to the call to prayer, *kiran sallah*, as they called it. Even in his semi-wakefulness, he wondered how a people of such religious zeal could be this traditional. At first, he had thought the story he would write of them would be a complete tale of religious extremism and all. He had had plans of writing a tragedy he was sure he would be inspired for, here. Now, with this, he knew the genre was going to be comedy! Who'd have thought that these people of the far North would be as superstitious as his Christian grandmother in the East? Mama would offer gifts to the gods and perform all the usual rituals. She would pull their ears reminding them of all the traditions. With Mama there was no waking on the wrong side of the bed. She believed that waking up on the left side of the bed brought bad luck. Because of this, she never rose at once. If she became conscious from sleep on the left side, she would wait a few minutes, force sleep then somehow make sure she rose from the right side. Tombo had never understood how she got to this. All her children—and grandchildren except Tombo, of course—had grown to follow her in this and a few of her other ways. However, Tombo always noted the side he woke up on, but kept it strictly to the bed. On those occasions when he had cause to sleep in the open like once when he did in the garage, his mind never paid attention to the side he woke up on. There were several other things Mama would do in reverence of tradition, her superstitions and the ancestors. After all these, she would be the first to go for morning mass each day and Sunday. She never missed tithing and was a big mother there.

A certain sense told him to go to the river. He ignored it.

He closed his eyes as he felt a hand shaking him. He was on the left side. He opened his eyes and noted that the sun had sneaked into the room in its full splendour. *Had he slept that long?* It was Lateef.

"Tombo, please can I have the twenty thousand naira I *lent* you?"

"Okay." He searched the pockets of his boxer shorts. Wasn't that where he had kept it the previous night? Okay, maybe the money was in his trouser. Yes, that had to be it. He stood up from the bed to go and get the money. The trend of events since the *borrowing* was amazing. He had *collected* that money when things were rough. To repay, he had been forced to save his entire allowance for the month in addition to begging a lot of people around. He knew he was going to have to go begging for the next month too. "Damn. I will never *borrow* money in my life again." A frown appeared on his face as he searched the fourth and final pocket of his trouser.

"What?!"

"Tombo, what is it?"

Tombo searched his pocketless t-shirt. His predicament became apparent to Lateef:

"Tombo, I need my money now! If I don't get it, I will deal with you. You stole that money from me and I told you to pay back. You begged me to give you some time which I have done. If you don't return it, I will bring the police for you. I hear that writers write better in prisons. I guess you will soon be finding that out first hand. Get me my money!"

Tombo knew who Lateef was and didn't want his trouble. It was like putting one's hand into fire. It would only take Lateef's reporting to their Local Government Inspector, the person in charge of all Corp members. That would be the end as Tombo would be stripped of his khaki, their uniform. It would be the worst ignominy. His mind jogged to all the places he had been to the previous day. He remembered putting the money in the pocket of his boxer shorts... The river came to his mind. He grabbed his t-shirt and ran all the way. He got to the river and walked around slowly. He searched around but found nothing. It was the community washing day and there were people around. Anyone might have taken it. He asked around but no one understood what he was talking about. He left them and rushed to the bushes where he had settled to do his business the previous night. He frantically searched for his faeces. The money had to be beside it. He was certain it had fallen when he had been scared by a frog. He saw his faeces. How he knew it, is hard to know. He jumped in excitement:

"Yes!!" and rushed towards it. He stepped on fresh faeces on the ground, but was oblivious of it. He searched around but found nothing. A small crowd was gathering; Tombo didn't seem to notice. He searched frantically around. No, that wasn't his *excreta*! Perhaps, it was the other one in the distance. "Yes!!" He rushed to it and scattered it searching for the money. Tombo's shirt went off as the sweat started to increase in his search. They all stared on, wondering what was wrong with him. How had this handsome man become mad all of a sudden? Not a few people were conversant with his stance on traditions and all. But still, it was hardly known that one would be punished for not believing. Then, someone came and mentioned that Tombo had been seen coming to the river on the previous night. Many shook their head in understanding and pity as the young man kept searching every fresh faeces around.

Lateef soon found his way to the scene with the police. By this time, Tombo was stark naked, searching for the right excreta. Lateef was shocked to immobility. There was Tombo, with scattered hair, and searching on. There was a look of glee and anxiety on his face too. The police, the crowd and all, looked on. It was another lesson to one and all.

The gods had won, once more...

* * *

He felt his heart stop. There was darkness. Complete darkness. Then like a fluid transition, a different darkness. A mosquito stole its pint. He didn't swipe at it. He heaved in relief. He was on the left side. He forced his consciousness away...

By dawn, he was a convert.

WHEN TIME COMES TO CALL

One of those days found Timbir taking his usual one-to-two hour walks. He marvelled at the number of cars in the city. Only three years ago, a walk down this same road would have encountered a countable number of very predictable cars. He waved to the cook at the corner, working to meet the teeming demands of her ever increasing customers. She shot him a look of acknowledgement from a window, and continued with her work. These days, she had no time to even wave back. That was a big change. There was the time when she would cook only once and have leftovers to spare at the end of the day. In those days, Timbir would go in and chat with her. They would talk about anything and everything. He knew how many stories he had been inspired to write from simply talking to her. There was her son who had a calabash for a stomach who would have to wait for the leftovers;

"Uncle, buy me this." "Buy me that." "Thank you, Uncle." Very warm boy who made Timbir feel like a biological uncle. Who would have guessed they were from two different regions of the country? Such was the warmth. The last time he had seen the boy, there had been noticeable change. The boy had grown up as had the warm "Uncle." Timbir was now "Sir" in a very polite tone. He heard that the young man was in a very big school now. He missed the boy. It was also one of the benefits of the new times; politeness over warmth. He smiled at the woman busy at work, in a proper suit, giving instructions to her workers in this big building. Who would believe this was the same person he had called cook?

He continued on his way, stopping at the church; a big magnificent edifice. He remembered the previous years. People used to fellowship in the pastor's two bedroom flat. It was a common sight, then, to find groundnuts in the offertory box. All the times he had passed the area had made him laugh. The pastor had always told him to be wary, saying that the parable of the mustard seed remained.

"Perhaps, for your grandchildren!" Timbir had retorted each time with both of them laughing. These days only crisp currency notes lined the box. The pastor had grown from the slim happy faced man to a fat, clownish person; an exploiting smile at his lips each time. He no longer visited Timbir. His visits were reserved for the bigger houses of the faithful. The business of the church now took priority and even the spare time of the shepherd had to be spent in more favourable investments. The prophecy of the mustard seed had sure come to pass. Timbir shook his head. Things had moved fast and the whole country had changed in a whiff.

He continued his walk and eventually got to his car, someone on his trail. The beggar came in his tattered clothes and flagged Timbir down. He looked at the beggar and turned his face away. He climbed into his Highlander jeep and thought of how different things had become. It was no longer a communal society and even family had become distant. He engaged the gears and ignited his car to life, raising the dust into the face of the man now left behind. His brother, in his ragged clothes, looked on as Timbir drove off. It was the sign of the times.

LUAMBA'S BATTLE

Luamba stared blankly into the half-empty glass that sat beside the bottle. He seemed lost in the million bubbles that danced around. After a few more minutes, he cradled the glass and guided it to maybe its hundredth oscillation to his lips. Beside his current half bottle sat three compatriots drained of their glory. There was an extra one unopened. Somewhere ahead, someone was shouting. It seemed he had been talking for some time:

"The government is funny *na*... The President is going to pick a new private jet for the First Lady. I know. Very soon, all the Governors will be asking for *their* own. Is that not how they decided to arm all the nomads in the North? It is the traditional rulers that are doing it. They are collaborating with the government to give the idiots arms. If only our boys had weapons..."

"Are you telling me? Which weapons? That's how the boys will take it to finish everyone off. Nobody goes to church anymore. Even those who go, do so for show. When church was church, everyone's truth could be seen in their lives. Give me that ol' time religion *jare*!"

"But with the way things are going, it seems there is no difference between any of the leaders o..."

They were talkative. It seemed that the beer had gotten to their heads. Luamba returned his attention to the glass. Like a robot he downed what was left of his current bottle. His mind went to several issues. He came to a few minutes later and discovered the extra bottle beside his fourth bottle was empty. *When did I finish it?*

"Bar man! Bar man! One... one... once more..." A loud belch

punctuated the order. He looked to the man seated on the table beside him. *How? Where did he come from? When did he appear?* The man looked as if he had the world on his shoulders. *What did he know about the cares of the world?*

"My brother, this one you are carrying your face like a goat that just heard that it will make the Christmas pepper soup... You think you have problems? Hmmm. Wait first *na*."

The silent man looked at him with eyes that said 'Do NOT disturb'.

This one is probably one of those ones who think they are better than others. He thinks he is a worse sufferer. What does he know?

"My brother, you have a bag at least. Me, I don't have anything. Just a medallion; a small charm of life. Wait, are you waiting for someone? Are you a stranger here? Excuse me... Bar man! Bar man! Where's this barman? He's probably called Barnabas, eh? *Ho ho ho ha ha ha*. Must be... I once had a friend called Barnabas but I am not sure I have any friends any more. There's too much strife in this life. Barnabas! One more beer here!

"You are a stranger here, I see. Your load more than says it all. Listen still, if you will. She... Don't you want to know who she is? Well, does it matter? *Any ways*, she gave me just enough transport to go back to the village. Thank you, Barnabas. To go to all ... all that poverty, to a hopelessness. C'mon! Please, Barnabas, bring another bottle for my friend here.

"What? You shake your head. You don't want a drink? Then, by all means, take some meal or whatever you want, please. There's little or nothing to life than a celebration of now. Tomorrow is a parcelled box that might turn out a gift or bomb! *Ho ho ho ha ha ha!*"

Luamba studied the man more. Whatever lay at the bottom of his heart was heavy. *Why allow any weight make one sink when you can sail on a bottle of Star to heights unknown?*

"My brother, there's nothing that Star cannot kill o! One bottle! Barnabas!"

The man seemed to be shifting away slowly. Luamba kept the distance close. He felt a vibration and brought out his phone from his pocket:

"Ah! It is my sister. Hello... Yes... You threw me out, why do you want to know? ... Well, not as if you care but I am in the Sewuese Bush Bar...Yeah? ... But seriously, can I come back and leave tomorrow? You know it's late... Okay, don't worry! I shall NOT come back again or beg you for money! ... It is my life and my money! ... Transport? ... Let me tell you something ... Hello? ... Hello? ... Abeg! ... Bye!" He turned back to the man. "Yes... *belch* Don't fidget like that. If ... Don't fidget like that. If you wish for nothing, at least ... Here, take. Keep this little gift. You need it more. For me, I will go home. My friend, I will go home. I will go home. I only find it sad that I will not be able to take anything to my fiancée and all *those my* little cousins. While I was away, they might have been content and kept hoping. You know, the little children used to call me Daddy. Daddy, when you come back, we will get books to write in school. We will get uniform and stop wearing this tear-tear. *Hmm...* Friend, there is hope. There is hope. I will go to the village. There might be no farms in a land desecrated by oil spillage or no fish in waters flowing with chemical slime. Still, there is hope and I will cultivate that hope. Indeed, many times, a glorious surplus has germinated from hope's harvest." There seemed to be tears in the stranger's eyes now. He was shaking. *Ah! At least there are people who have hearts in this world. But a man shouldn't cry jare.* "My brother, your eyes are red. Wipe them. Remember hope! Life's essence is a continuous reliance on hope. It only ends at the final darkness. Whoever said Naijaria will not overcome evil is a liar. My brother, I say the devil is a liar! Halleluiah!"

"Amen!" shouted the man from the other table who had started talking about churches. "That's my man! I didn't know there were believers here! I like people who don't mind to speak up their religion. I was a Pastor too, you know? I was...is...am Pastor..."

"Pastor Green Bottle!" his mate concluded for him and the bar fell into a bout of laughter.

Luamba stood up to go and shake Pastor Green Bottle. That table seemed to be the happening table. He looked back to discover his mate rushing out of the bar:

"We will not have stolen the bag o!" someone threw after the man.

This drew more laughter.

There was a loud explosion and suddenly, all was still.

*

The bodies were burnt, some beyond recognition. Tears poured freely from Bargo's eyes as she recognised the medallion that was held firmly in what must have been the corpse's hand. The medallion or what remained of it. She had bought it from Tony, a course mate of hers.

"It is indestructible." Tony had told her all those years ago.

"Are you sure?"

"Yes *na*. It was my grandfather that gave it to me. I have ten of them. My grandfather was the greatest artefact maker in the whole wide world! I swear! In fact, if not that I don't have any money to complete my school fees, do you think I would have wasted my time even talking to you now?"

She had looked at him and then at the medallion. It was a beauty quite okay. Even if it wasn't going to last forever, she was sure she would use it for long. Again, she had the opportunity of helping Tony out. She handed him the money he had requested for.

"Thank you! God bless you overdose! God bless you plentifully! It is for good luck. The person that owns it will be protected. God save us!"

Luamba had turned to a piercing pine, a distraction with his lack of focus. How could he have turned out to be so wayward? Her only brother! She had escaped to the city and hustled till she made headway. She had struggled through life and was constantly harassed by her brother's letters of how she had forsaken him. When she made some headway in life, she had gone to the village to pick him up. Bargo had given him the medallion:

"I think you will need far more of the good luck," she had said, ending the tale of the medallion to the skinny boy as he got prepared for a new life. They had both laughed. "Keep this card on you always too."

"What is it for?" He had asked looking at the square complimentary card she gave him. "I know your number offhand *na*. I can even call it from my sleep."

"I know. It is in case of emergency. Someone can use it to call me as your next of kin."

"Ah! Nothing can happen to me o! Okay. I would keep it and my luck charm."

He had settled in well and she had toiled her life out for the both of them. After years of sacrificing for him, he had decided to pay her back with evil. She had arranged to have him married to the daughter of one of her bosses; a fine lady. Luamba had the audacity to take a preference for a village woman on the pretence of love! Not in her house! To make matters worse, he decided to drop out of the university with the excuse that he wanted to focus squarely on painting! How could a third year student of Classical Literature and Philosophy quit a year to graduation?

What? Bargo had pleaded all she could and when she discovered that Luamba wasn't prepared to think straight, she had shown him the way out. Only this morning... As he stepped out, he told her that he would hold on to her medallion no matter what...

He kept his word. An intense feeling of guilt rushed from within streaming slowly out of her eyes. She looked on but saw nothing. She held the charred fingers wondering at the black figure that lay in front of her. Suddenly, it didn't matter that he had decided to drop out or wanted to become a painter or even rubbish packer. All she wanted was her brother back.

If only... Kai... So, I forsake him once more, even in death. Why? Why?

Why?

The last call played back in her mind; she had been rude. She had shouted at him and told him he was useless and incapable of finding the road to anything positive in life. She was infuriated that she had given him only his transport fare and his feet had found the bar. How could she have known that an hour later the vicinity of the same bar would be the location of the blast reported on TV?

If only... It brought back memories of her best friend, Doremi, who had been admitted in the hospital for AIDS. The once chubby Doremi had become a skeleton with near empty sockets where bulgy eyes had once sat. Bargo decided she didn't want to see her friend that way or remember her as such. She stopped visiting. The doctors said Doremi had died far earlier than she was meant to, depressed. Bargo wore guilt deep, wondering if it wasn't her neglect that had killed her friend. And now, there was Luamba. Was she so bad she always let those she loved to die?

Bargo found a corner, sat on the floor, hugged her knees and let the tears stream down. Her phone began to vibrate. She wondered who was calling. She let it ring thrice. She picked at the caller's fourth try.

Sniff Sniff "Yes? ... Speaking ... What is it?! ... Yes, I am there ... You want me to come and take my brother's dead body? ... Hmm? ... Yes, I am the woman in the red dress? What?..."

* *

"*Kai!*" She covered her mouth to shield her instant cry as she caught sight of the figure on the bed. The skin was open in several parts, burns decorating spots that were left open while bandages covered up every other part. There was a machine and blood at a corner dripping through a line to his hands. It was more than she could take. She rushed out and pushed past the throngs of people around. The President was around on a sympathy visit. He walked fast as if he did not want to stay longer than he ordinarily should. She thought of her brother and the apparition she had seen on the bed. Then, she remembered her anguish at his supposed loss, remembered Doremi and knew she had to go back.

She walked into his room, stepped to his bedside and placed a kiss on what remained of his forehead.

THE PEN AND SWORD

You raise your thoughts to the highest heavens, even though you are at your lowest. You drink of the wonders of so much written, yet find no merit to quench the thirst that is drinking you up. You hear more words, and see much more evils...

What should be, what should be?

The puzzles turn on and on, tumbling about in your head till your every thought becomes a mass of unanswered questions, much like wires turned loose.

You have stopped watching TV; you have stopped reading the news; you have struggled to leave the world. But somehow, the troubles still get to you. The news you refuse to find, the realities of the time.

You pick your pen to put into action once more the ink everyone marvelled at. You want to bleed out all the evils that have now become a monster in you.

It flows and you smile, but not for long as you find more of those villains coming to get your people. You discover that your leaders are complicit...

Then you go to Opi, kiss the forked junction and remember that one who wore the eagled insignia. You pick his mantle and make the sign of the cross.

Suddenly, you realize you no longer believe that the pen is mightier than the sword.

HALF MAST

...the other ends a dot
the pain a river, unique
uniting us all
in our deepest hidden hope
for each other's final fall...

The night betrayed the tension that hung on the various members like ropes. The crickets sang shrill songs as toads croaked codes no one could comprehend. One after the other, the men and women took their seats in the large hall by the riverside; their traditional meeting place.

Bondigo presided over the meeting. His face was set, grim–it always was. He allowed them to keep talking. Usually a voting session could be put off if the Supremo—Bondigo—asked that the members let things be. There was a silent clause to it: if anyone raised an objection, the vote would go on. Then, it would come to the lifting of flags: black or white; for or against. Bondigo's single hope was to ensure it didn't come to that. If they spoke long, they would lose track or he would distract them...

"The blood still boils. It seems that the log has finally stayed in the water so long that it has become a crocodile."

"It has not reached that..."

"Did you see the papers? Billions of cash to the East because of the small flood... None to us."

"The billions he spent on independence *nko?*"

"The plan was always to get one of us in there," Bondigo said in his booming voice. "We should be honoured to have one of our own there."

"Of what use is living by the river if the waters are poisoned?"

"He was just a scheming arsehole. He never had our interest."

"Enough! No more! There shall be no move!" Bondigo's eyes bulged red in the intimidating way he had perfected to make sure no one raised any opposition. It was his way of stamping 'Final!' It was the traditional way of ending every dispute. No one ever raised an opposition. There was always silence...

"Opposed."

Bondigo couldn't believe it: "Wha... what?" He looked to his farthest left at the speaker, the President's paternal uncle... The man wasn't done yet:

"When water stays in the mouth too long, it becomes spittle. Perhaps he has stayed too long. The President is our son, but we need to move on."

"But he is our son..."

"He is our son but stopped being *one of us* when he became bigger than the cabal and all of us."

A uniform nodding of heads around showed approval. Only the Supremo could raise the motion for the vote. All the eyes around challenged their leader. He sighed:

"Black flags for making the move to attack; white flags for ignoring the moves—and making peace with the President, who is one of us."

Of all the flags brought forward, only one was white.

Three days later, the country's flag flew at half mast.

IF EVERYDAY WERE CHRISTMAS

I t was not the best of times. It was the war. The soldiers shuffled on. The weariness of docile inactivity had long started to take its toll. Feet dragged unyielding bodies.

"Move!" came the single shout of the Captain, Chris. It could not be easily described what the word signified. It lacked the bark of an order; though the loudness indicated it was directed at the men. Somehow it registered to a few as a word of encouragement. Minions repeated it automatically through cracked lips that had long defeated every form of moistening. The words hardly registered to many others as the trudge continued. Chris sighed.

She was the leader of this unit, one of the few lady soldiers in the whole army. They all called her 'Sir.' Some said her name had gotten her in and once in, she couldn't be let go—she was that good. Headquarters always seemed to be rotating her. The war seemed to be a definer of times like a new calendar. There was a life before; now—the war; and the hope of a life after. In the life before, she had been a writer, and mother. She looked forward to the life after when she would get back to it. She was thinking of the book she was going to write as soon as the war was over. She was more of a poet but she would look into fiction this time. So much to say that the *thickly* thin lines of poetry full of their overstretched meanings would not deliver in exact words. There truly was more than enough to last a world. *If every single thing that she did, or that happened was to be written, not all the books in the world would be able to contain it.*

She thought of her soldiers. Any fire of enthusiasm in the glory of patriotic bloodletting was long turned ash in the visual dots that hardly stayed open in the dust all around. Days without activity, food or water had long left them wondering what battle they faced. The battle seemed now with the elements and nature. It appeared that hunger could easily have conquered any of these sooner than any enemy's bullet. Differing their varying skin shades or clothing, the men were uniformly brown. This was the harmattan's cloak put on them all. It added to their gloom. The despair was contagious. To avoid its infection, she allowed her mind dart to the individual stories of the soldiers she remembered. Many times in those cold moments, it was the various stories that warmed her and kept her fit. Sometimes she refreshed her mind on briefs. Kabuza came to her mind.

She spotted him and shook her head. It seemed he had been changing units with her. The man did not have the interest of the war at heart. Everyone knew this. He was simply a zombie. The story of his recruitment was interesting. No one knew how the story originated but it had passed around long and steady that it had grown to wear the toga of fact. It was two years ago. The man had been hiding with his son in the bush. After some days of hunger they both chanced on a chameleon, as the story went. Who killed it was not clear as both had stoned it at the same time. The chameleon was small and might have been overlooked by a father for a hungry son. Both of them grabbed the dead reptile as father glared at son, asking total submission. Submission and obedience were for the life before. The thirteen year old was no longer a boy. He threw the first punch as Kabuza dodged. It turned into a hot fight that nearly left the boy dead. That was meant to teach the child a lesson. In his triumph, the father seized the chameleon and started eating it. He was halfway through when he realized what had just happened. He looked to his son with the shame in his eyes and offered the boy what remained of the prize. The boy later disappeared, joining the army—it seemed—to find a way to deal with his father. It was more than he could take so Kabuza ran to the recruitment office and offered his services, searching for his son while exchanging units.

Chris still looked at him as he brought something out of his pocket and cleaned it. She noted it was a picture. She would have asked whose it was but Kabuza was said to have a violent temper. He was also said to be mentally unstable. Everyone tried to steer clear of him. Chris had been properly briefed on that one. It was strange though, that he seemed to follow every single command. Yes, that was another thing: *His instinct is his main asset and is the reason he is still in the army*, the report had also said. With the shortage of soldiers and volunteers, who dared retrench any full bodied soldier? It wasn't as if this unit was an elite one either. There were a few original soldiers but their numbers here were negligible. The greatest number of these types, who kept reducing each day, had been posted to the main command. Most of her soldiers were volunteers and former civilians—like herself—whom the necessity of the times had forced a uniform on. Chris shook her head.

*

It was the seventh day of their journey as the soldiers came across a village. It was deserted. With the times, such places had become a normal sight. Chances of finding anything were usually slim. Desertion usually meant either fleeing or killed people. It was a usual prayer that the inhabitants would have fled rather than be killed. This was not due to any charity but practical wisdom. It was somewhat confusing, the idea behind it but practical enough. A village of dead people was ready testimony an army had passed through that town. No army would pass on without plundering. Fleeing people however usually left food in their hurry. A lucky unit or army could get something. It seemed that this village was a mixture of both. A quick look in some of the huts revealed some provisions. In seconds everyone was aware. The excitement in the air belied the mummies that had been walking on before. Caution was a word existent no more. They took their fill of what they could and didn't notice the changing face of the sky. They soon found dark descending on them. It wasn't long before it became stark.

"We are camping the night here, Sir!" A majority of the soldiers declared as if they had had a meeting. Chris told them to hold still as she would look to make sure the place was safe. There was no taking chances. There might have been no activity but this wasn't any other time—it wasn't like *before*. She was in charge of everyone's life. She knew that she would have loved them to continue with the journey into the night and on. Still, she *loved* her men more and knew they were exhausted. This part usually took sway in all her reasoning. Against her natural judgment, Chris knew she was going to agree. She moved around, inspecting the area. She saw a hut that would suit her purposes for that night. The harmattan winds whistled sweetly. There was something surprisingly pleasant about the air. Sometimes, the war could have strange effects on people. *It was especially so when the fighting was so far away.* She noted a soldier running, a trophy in his hand.

"Bring it here." Chris called to the soldier.

It was a digital watch. The soldier had got it from one of the other huts they had already started plundering. She handed the watch back to the soldier, uninterested.

"*Sah!*"

"Yes?"

"*Sah*, you no see date?" He asked, smiling. It was strange. That was something you hardly saw on the field. She ignored it. The soldier handed the watch back to his Captain. It declared 25:12 20:01:45. One minute past Eight, Twenty-Fifth December. Then, it hit her. Chris smiled. The times had become so abnormal that people forgot dates, even Christmas. In ordinary times she might not have given it much thought but now its significance seemed like a miracle. Had it really been months since the war started? She wondered if it was going to end at all. She looked at her watch to confirm the date. It was truly so.

"Tell the soldiers to take the night off and get fully refreshed. We are moving ahead after that, full throttle. Meanwhile, tell the sentry—lookout guards, and scouts to take position. Tell their replacements to be on the alert to replace them as soon as their shift ends. Let the Sergeant ensure this. Is that clear? Good. One more thing: Merry Christmas, kid." The boy, who could not have been more than sixteen, smiled back.

"*Tank* you Sah!" He ran out of the hut, remembered something, and rushed back in. Chris raised her head up immediately. The soldier banged his right foot and saluted, "Sorry, *Sah!*" A relieved Chris chuckled to the boy's embarrassment. The exaggerations, especially on the parts of these ones, were usually the comic relief that one needed in this sort of world where everything was so serious and fast. Noting after a while that his superior was only amused, not disgusted, the boy chuckled back and ran out again.

If only everyday could be Christmas, both of them must have thought at that moment. Her mind went to a younger boy who had been in her former platoon; a teenager! He was of the opposing camp and had been captured. These were not the sort of prisoners that they needed! Still, she spoke to the boy and discovered that the boy's father was a university don. What amazed her was that the boy had no interest in books. His was a life of adventure, even at that tender age.

"Wars are not for children," the Captain had cautioned often. She had been harsh and tried all means to send the boy away from the camp. The boy had his mind made up already. He stuck on like the camp had been made for him. Somehow, with time, the boy and the Captain got attached like mother and child. Her mission for the boy changed with this affection.

Chris had tried to teach him to see the beauty of books. To teach him the basic three L's; literature, love and life, was the plan. There wasn't so much for him to do then, and there was some time on their side. It was a bit like the present moment; dull without much activity on their paths. Still, there were some occasional encounters and killings. The idealistic boy was soon brainwashed and was more of the soldiers than they, themselves. The boy became full of zest and longing for blood; that of his people! This was before the boy's conversion or turning point, as Chris always thought of it.

The night of the turning point was fresh in her mind.

On that rare occasion, their spies had spotted enemies a little distance ahead. Exhausted, they decided to camp the night before advancing on the enemies the next day. Not the boy. He had wandered out to seek the 'enemies' alone. At roll call, he was found absent. There was no difficulty guessing where he would be. A search party went after him, Chris in its lead. It took a while but eventually, he was found, slightly wounded. The boy was crying, a silenced gun in his hand. Not far off, a dead man was seen. Realities sometimes turn out for children, and truly all, to mean something different from ideals. It wasn't as fun as the boy had thought it would be. He was taken to the medics. The boy had no more taste for blood and shuddered often like a drenched chicken in harmattan. A willing student now, Chris taught him when she found the time.

She later found a way to sneak the boy out:

"Make sure you learn how to read and write to perfection. Keep in touch," she whispered as she watched him disappear into the night. The boy headed back to his father's house but found his whole town scarred. The sight of a woman with a *rottening* stomach troubled him. The boy explained in the letter he sent to Chris that her distended abdomen suggested that she had been pregnant. Both mother and child were dead now. He always wondered what the child might have grown up to be in the future. There were the bodies of little children in almost every shelter one could find. Crippled and injured people, physically and mentally, filled the land. The war was evil on both the war and civilian fronts. There was hardly any distinction between the two anymore.

The boy with luck had found his way out of the country with some missionaries, health workers or like organization. He had not been clear on this aspect. Still, he continued, if all went as he planned he would become a medical doctor. He would also become a writer.

She folded the boy's letter which she had instinctively brought out. She put it in her trouser pocket and brought out her wallet. She took out a picture. It was that of her daughter as a baby, five years old now. She ran her hand over the image and smiled. Chris wondered if she would see her daughter again. She closed her eyes and imagined what would have happened if things had been different, if she were home at that moment. A few tears came to her eyes. She hurriedly brushed them off. She got inspiration and stepped out of her temporary quarters. There was great gaiety in the air. The good humour of the camp had come back. They had somehow found a water source and incredibly, wine. The announcement that it was Christmas had long made the rounds and as it seemed, a party was in progress.

Soldiers indeed, she thought to herself. *They are more of children who Santa has given gifts and for all the world, what if that is what has happened?*

They hailed her. She acknowledged with a nod and moved on. She sought the soldier and found him. He was still fingering the photograph she had seen earlier on.

"Kabuza!"

"Sir!"

"Why are you alone by that fire?"

"Everyone seems to ignore me. The only ones who ever tried to come near me only taunted me...Sir."

Chris was shocked, not only at the man's answer but his command of English. Hadn't she been properly briefed that the man was mad and of a bad temper, only good for instinct?

"Why are you not celebrating with the others?" Chris asked again, as if she had not heard Kabuza's reply, at the same time pointing to the other soldiers who jollied around. There was a pause.

"You believe I am mad, right?"

Chris had no words. She did not seem to notice that the man had dropped the 'Sir': "What?"

"Do you have any children, Ma'am?"

"Kabuza, are you asking me a question?"

"Yes. Do you have any children?"

Something in the quietness of his voice touched her:

"Yes, a daughter. Five...I hope." She said, passing her daughter's picture to Kabuza, as she sat down beside him: "Kabuza?"

"She is pretty. Too bad she is going to be an orphan soon. I am not sure if any of us would survive this, you know." He handed back the picture and looked directly into Chris's eyes. Now the Captain felt uneasy.

"You must have heard of my son and how I killed him... No, you don't have to say a word, Ma'am. I have never tried to disprove anyone's tale because no one asked me. I let them humour themselves.

39

There is a different story to it. In reality, he—my son—left our house one stormy night. It was the first Christmas of the war. Things weren't so bad then. We were also assured then, that things would come to an end soon. This Christmas makes it two. It was before our town was crushed. He simply dropped a note saying that he was gone to join the army."

"Just like that? What was his reason?" Chris asked.

"No reason but the crazy adventure of youth." Kabuza replied and shook his head slowly, "He had such hot blood. My wife saw the note first. She collapsed and died in that instant, shock I think. She was hypertensive, you know. The magic of the moment was lost on me. It was Christmas day. They were my Christmas. I picked my things soon after and enrolled into the army. I sought information of my son changing camps with whatever help I could get. I soon got information that he had been killed. I felt bitter and knew I could never be the same. I died in the knowledge becoming a thing without a focus, you know. I lost sight of the cause and eventually found out I did not know who I was fighting with or against. I have changed camps so much I do not seem to know the difference anymore, you know. I am now an instinct man, killing whoever the enemy of my camp is. I prefer your command though and so I have stayed long, silently." He ended his story: "Oh, here is his picture."

He proffered the picture he had been fingering all through to Chris. Chris stretched her hand to collect the picture. Kabuza withdrew the picture as he noticed the fire had nearly died out. He tried to adjust it but discovered that the wood was not enough. He stood up to search for more dry wood around. He came back shortly and fixed them into the fire. Quite soon, the fire was rekindled.

"There you are. Sorry about that. Yes, here is the picture."

Chris collected the picture slowly this time, in case Kabuza wanted to take it back. No withdrawal. She looked at it. Her eyes narrowed a bit as she adjusted the picture to look at it properly in the light of the fire;

"Jude?"

"Sorry? Yes. Eh... I didn't mention his name... What? You know him?!"

Chris smiled. It was the son of the university don,

"This is your son?" Kabuza simply nodded, wide-eyed, "You must be Professor Black."

"Yes. Now, don't call me Kabuza again!" the professor said, a thrill in his voice to cushion the joke, as a smile absent from his face since a long time back appeared. He seemed to relax a bit. All of a sudden, his face assumed its grimness again, "Tell me what you know. Quickly. Immediately..."

Chris looked at him, a bit angered at the tone he was using. The imploring eyes held hers fast and begged in messages words could not translate. She calmed down and told the professor the story of his boy ending with where she thought the boy was and what he was up to. She gave the professor the letter. The man devoured its contents as if he had been starved of reading all his life. It was a thirsty parched person in the desert seeing water for the first time in two years. He roared, emitting a laugh from his belly:

"Ho ho ho! Ha ha ha ha! I can never thank you enough, Chris, eh, Ma'am...Sir. You have made me a happy man, you know. If I die today, I die a most happy death in knowledge of the magic of Christmas. Hey! You are a messenger of it. Chris, the child and preparer of the Christmas named for you. Ha! I don't know what to say. Ha!! Ha!! Ha!! Ha!! Ho!! Ho!! Hee..."

Chris opened her mouth to say something as a soldier approached at that point to tell the Captain that she was needed immediately. The radio had come alive; there was a message. The soldier wasn't surprised at the crazy laughter of Kabuza but was shocked to see his Captain in the man's company. Noting the seeming level of familiarity between them, he wondered if the Captain was not mad herself. *Well, with ladies, you could never tell.* Chris stood up to leave;

"Merry Christmas, Professor."

"Merry Christmas, Chris."

This time, Chris mentally noted that the 'Sir', 'Ma'am' and 'Captain' had left the soldier's address for her. She shook her head as she followed the soldier who had come to call. There was some serious action coming their way. *They were soon going to be in action, again.* She looked at her watch. It was 00:01. She smiled;

"If only everyday could be Christmas."

She shook her head again, walking to duty, thinking of the road ahead.

PUZZLES

Bule woke up with a start. Was that the sound of knock-outs? Knock-outs, bangers were rare in these parts and he wondered if he had heard right. Was that the sound of someone's cry too? Voices filtered through into his room. He opened the window and peered into the night, but there was nothing to see. Darkness had eaten the night and the shadows had pushed the moon out, as Baba would say. He wondered who these were talking at this time of the night. Perhaps Baba had visitors.

Back on his bed, he closed his eyes, grateful that he could go back to sleep.

KPOAAAAAAAA! KPOAAAAAAAA! KPOAAAAAAAA!

He froze where he lay, but his pulse quickened to the sound of his pounding heart. The noise sounded much closer and was not a loner like the first. His bed felt safer, yet curiosity would not allow him remain lying down. Each step towards the window made his heart pound even louder. The noise was from close by, over the low fence. A distant light outlined the silhouette of two groups of people: one set had objects in their hands, while the second group of men stood opposite the first—their hands placed on their heads.

There was that loud noise again, repeatedly, and this time anxious shouts followed. The group of men with their hands on their heads fell to the ground. Something was wrong!

Bule heard his father call his name.

"Baba!" He replied, praying everything was alright. His stomach churned and he felt cold. His father's voice sounded urgent;

"Where are you?"

No sooner than Bule appeared, his father snatched him into his hands and ran straight out of the door into the night.

"Baba, where are we going?"

All that occupied his father's mind was escape. He gave no reply but sprinted on like a man whose feet were fit with wings while carrying his son. A cloud of dust rose into the stale night air, every moment Baba's running feet pounded into the earth. Looking behind, Bule noticed a noisy crowd. The crowd was running towards them. Noise coming towards them, from another direction, made him turn. It was another crowd heading their way. Bule's eyes bulged. He began to tremble in his father's arms. What was wrong with all the adults? His father's arms tightened around him. Baba was sweating. He ran with no destination in mind.

The crowd got closer. Bule could see their arms and hands, raised in a menacing manner; waving about in the air, wielding different types of long black objects and some shiny short ones. Their voices sounded angry and aggressive.

Bule's father ran even faster. He did not know in what direction to flee, but his added strides belied that confusion. He did not want the crowd coming behind to catch up with them; neither did he want to fall into the hands of the oncoming crowd. He ran towards a bushy path leading nowhere, guided by the light from father moon slowly being covered by a gathering cloud.

They arrived at a building Bule did not recognise. Baba put him down and tried the door. It would not budge. Baba cursed. Bule gasped and his mouth fell open; he had never heard his father curse before. Baba picked him up in a hurry. He had to keep on running.

Baba barely took two steps forward before that loud noise rang out once again. Baba fell forward like a felled *dogon-yaro* tree, almost on top of Bule. His body convulsed. To Bule, his father was doing a strange dance, lying with his face to the side, in the dirt.

There were jubilant cries from the mob. Bule looked away from them towards his father. The clouds gave way to the moon's illumination at that moment and his eyes fell to the increasing puddle of blood that gathered around his father's chest.

"Baba!" Bule screamed as his hands trembled.

Baba raised his head up from the dirt.

"Run away! Always remember…" he struggled to say. Baba looked at his son and forgetting his pain for a second, smiled. There was hope as long as the young ones were left. He started again, "Always remember…"

That loud noise struck again:

KPOAAAAA!!

Baba's struggling voice ceased in horror as he saw his son fall limp.

"Baba!" Bule's face contorted in pain. His tiny frame did the same dance as his father's. This time he did not need anyone to explain what had happened; the encroaching darkness said it all. He felt firm hands pick him up and rush. There was no sound. From within the darkness, he felt the deepest peace. But it wasn't his time, yet.

TRAILING ON DANGER'S TAIL

The Mother

The school gates usually closed at seven-forty a.m. It was seven-thirty. Karen checked the open engine once more. There didn't seem to be any problem with the car. She got back into the car and turned the key in the ignition. The car ignored her. Karen looked at her two sons in the back passenger seat. They looked angelic in their crisp uniforms. Their faces told a different story with deep frowns etched on both:

"Mummy, they will not allow us into school *o* and today is test."

She smiled reassuringly at Terry, her older son and went to the bonnet. She touched this and that, still without a clue as to what was wrong with the vehicle.

"Moooommmmmmy!" This time it was Tertimbir. She recognised the tears rising in his voice. She sighed and flagged down an oncoming commercial bike.

"U nder ve e?" the man greeted in her native Tiv. She was impressed.

"U nder nena?" she replied, enquiring how he was, "Please, take my children to Swenti Nursery and Primary school. How much do I pay you?"

"Fifty naira."

She gave him a hundred naira. He brought out his wallet to fish out her change but she waved it aside. She hugged her sons as she lifted them each to the bike seat. It took some effort; they sure had grown.

"I promise your food *would* be ready when you come back, okay?"

"Mummy, *will* it be spaghetti?" Terry asked.

"Yes, it will be spaghetti…"

"With plenty meat?" this one from Tertimbir.

"Yes, dear; spaghetti with plenty meat!"

The children were grinning now. Her smile grew broader, then she remembered and added:

"Make sure you eat during break, you hear?"

They both nodded. As the motorcycle sped away, she mentally noted the bike's plate number. She got her cell phone out and called her electrician. Fortunately, he was close by. He came and with a few touches, gave life to the car.

"What was wrong?"

"It wasn't anything much. *Ba damua* – no problem. You will not have any problem again. But call me if you have any more difficulties *sha*."

Karen paid him, got into her car and drove home.

School

Mr. Okon was one of those headteachers who usually stayed in school long after everyone had gone to ensure every record had been kept right. He had gone through the various class attendance registers and was now deep in work supervising the various notes from each form teacher. He wasn't impressed with most of what he saw. He eased his tie. It seemed he was going to have to stay longer to clear most of the *nonsense* that the staff had done. *The staff meeting for tomorrow is going to be really heated for them all*, he thought to himself. But how long would he go on like this? He needed to get some things going and fast. He could not keep telling his wife stories while other people made progress with jeeps and all. Well, that would come soon. For now, he had to pay attention to his job. He adjusted his glasses and was soon lost in his work.

There were two sharp raps on the door. He wondered who it could be. Maybe a teacher who had come to complain about something—*woe betide the person if it was any of the form teachers*. Or maybe the food seller with food. Ah! All the thoughts came in at the same thing but the last one got him smiling. He cleared his throat:

"Come in."

One of Mr. Okon's eyebrows arched up in displeasure as his eyes connected with the face of the entrant. Karen was not one of those parents who came in simply to say 'Hi.' She always had one issue or the other to complain about on how her children had been maltreated by this or that teacher. He rested his back into his chair and entwined his fingers in preparation for her definite challenge.

"Ah. Hello. Good afternoon, Mrs. Wergba. What is it with Terry and Tertimbir this time?"

"I was about to ask after them. I haven't seen them. They haven't returned yet."

"Returned? You took them somewhere?"

"No Sir, they came to school. I waited till four-thirty when the bus is meant to have brought them back. Their food was getting really cold and still no word. I came here after waiting thirty more minutes. I came to the school waiting room and found no one. I went to their classes but found the classes locked."

"Are you sure of this, Madam? You brought them here?"

Their faces became twin of the anxiety that lay in their hearts: "I personally sent..."

"Please, take a seat, Madam. What are their respective classes?"

She told him as he brought out two registers from among the files that were on his table. He checked the names and noted that zeros had been written there to signify the boys had been absent. He closed the second register as he raised up his head to her;

"Ma, they were abs... Mrs. Wergba!"

The Police

The haste with which the woman stepped into the station put the officers on the alert. She almost seemed to be the spirit of the wind that blew. She was directed to the right office and in no time, had three escorts with her. They drove to the secretariat of the commercial motorcyclists.

The sight of the armed police officers was enough to send the secretary into action. Some minutes later, they were able to identify the number of the plate that she had mercifully stored in her head, from a register.

"Na Igbazenda. I sabi where we fit see am." The secretary took the front passenger seat beside Karen who drove. The secretary turned out to be garrulous. As they drove on, he explained that Igbazenda was a recluse who didn't associate much with them. "I no go surprise if na him. But na pesin wey dey tek im taim."

"You no go surprise if na him do wetin?" one of the police officers asked.

It led to another story and on and on.

Karen hardly heard a word of what he was saying. She thought of her two children. *What on earth had happened to them? Where were they? God!* It had taken her ten years before she conceived. There had been a lot of pressure from her husband's family. She had been insulted and called all sorts of names from 'witch' to 'eater of children in her womb.' She had endured it all and kept praying, reminding God of Hannah in the bible. She had promised to put her first child in a Christian school right from his kindergarten stage. When the time came, it turned out that the Christian schools weren't good enough for her child.

"I will transfer them to the seminary. I promise." She said quietly as the tears threatened to break the banks of her eyes.

"But e fit be say im do accident." She turned to the secretary, wide eyed with sparks that showed shock and anger at his suggestion that Igbazenda might have had an accident with her children.

"God forbid!" She spat out with venom.

He looked at her and kept quiet till they got to the place they were heading to. They pulled over at a hut that the secretary had pointed at. It was a local bar. They all moved into the hut except for the secretary who took a bike back. They stepped into the bar and saw three men drinking palm wine. One of them was bare chest and seemed to have had a lazy day so far. Karen stepped in and in one glance, cognizance set in. It was Igbazenda, bare-chested:

"That is him!"

"What?"

"He is the one that took my children to school. He is the one!"

The police officers seized him.

"Wait! Wait! I am not the one – by my dead mother's grave! I am not the one, by Takur. I am not the one – by Akodo Gbaabua..."

"My friend, save it! You'll explain better in due time. Meanwhile, keep reciting the litany of your ancestors. You might need them to come and save you when we get to the station! Boys, pick him up!"

The Inspector

Inspector Tunde paced around his office, deep in thought. He rubbed his flat stomach in thought. Who would have thought that the Sociology Masters' degree holder would end up in the police force? Here he was. He had been in service for only five years but it had been really hectic. He was one of the best officers in the force. He always solved cases and remained one of those rare men who never took a bribe, who never condoned any criminal. He kept being transferred from one division to the other.

A constable walked into his office, stamped a foot in attention and thrust his chest forward in salute.

"Carry on."

"Oga Inspector, I sure say no be dis man do am. And im de tok say im dey thirsty."

"He said he is thirsty?"

"Yes, Sir."

It had been an hour since the interrogation started. Igbazenda kept swearing at *and by* this and that. He insisted that he had taken the children to school.

The inspector stepped out to the counter where Karen paced up and down. He had begged her to go and get some rest at home; that his men were on the job. He was sure it was a kidnap case.

"If it is ransom, I am ready to sell all I have and beg to any length. Please, tell him to tell you where my children are."

The inspector smiled. He was sure it wouldn't get to that. He would get the kids back. All she had to do was go and rest. He would contact her as soon as the man spoke. She wasn't listening. She paced up and down. They were fortunate she wasn't the wailing and rolling type. He had seen plenty of such cases. She looked up to him, a question asked in the silence:

"Not yet," he said as he came closer and noticed there were tears coursing down her face. He added feebly, "He will soon talk" and quickly walked back to his office, where the constable was waiting. "Do your job. Go back and give a cup of wonder juice to that man, compliments of the house. Then, call me and I will see if he is as innocent as he claims."

Igbazenda did not go past a sip of the fermented urine of the detainees of the station. It tasted worse than vinegar. He was allowed a few minutes more. Then the Inspector came in:

"Are you ready to talk?"

After a few minutes of a process that he knew best how to conduct, the question turned out to be the last time the inspector spoke. It was the first time Igbazenda spoke well.

Findings

The twin lights of the police van dotted through the darkness at full speed as they made their way to an unknown destination. It was midnight. Karen followed closely. Despite the chilly air rushing through the open windows, sweat glued her clothes to her body like the anxiety nearly drowning her. She mumbled her prayers as her hands worked down her chaplet on its fourth revolution. It seemed the journey wouldn't come to an end. Suddenly, in the other vehicle, Igbazenda's weary hand pointed to a warehouse-like building in the distance.

"Are you sure? You are not messing with our heads, right? You sure say you no dey mess with our head, *abi*?" one of the constables asked. Igbazenda nodded in affirmation.

The inspector smiled, "You better pray that this is not just a waste of my precious time. You are sure?"

Igbazenda nodded twice. The van pulled to a halt outside the building. Karen's car pulled up beside it shortly after. Inspector Tunde mentally noted that they had made a noisy entrance. He had already given his team their instructions. As they alighted, he walked straight to Karen's car. She was really stubborn. She had refused to stay back despite his warnings and threats. She had refused every order he had given and had only conceded to allowing a constable drive her. That was as far as his favours would go in this case. He was not going to allow her come in and jeopardize the operation. Igbazenda had said the house was empty but trust was too precious to be spent carelessly.

"Constable Gbatima, stay with her. Make sure she remains in the car." Karen began to protest but Inspector Tunde didn't wait to listen as he did a short jog and caught up with his officers. They took positions as Igbazenda led the way. He knocked on the door. With a rough poke from a constable, Igbazenda identified himself in answer to a question from within. The door opened cautiously as Inspector Tunde kicked the door. The door swung back within hitting the lady behind it. They rushed into the room and were greeted with gunfire. Inspector Tunde shot back in the direction of the fire. A grunt was heard. One of the officers rushed to where the lady was and secured her with handcuffs. She was sobbing already. A little tact ensured on the part of the police officers.

"Switch on the lights."

The lights came on. The warehouse was empty save for a few things scattered here and there. There was also a man who lay shot, a gun in his hand; the person Inspector Tunde had shot.

"Where are they? Lead the way, idiot!"

"I don't know where. I know say *na* here only."

"Bring the girl."

Without being told to, the girl led them to a door they hadn't noticed. They entered the room. The temperature of the room hit them. It was something of a cold room for preserving meat. There seemed to be some sacks in the corners.

"Switch on the lights here!"

Click! There was a huge stand at the farthest corner of the room and two sacks at the other.

"Where are they?"

The woman's shaky finger pointed to the sacks.

"Bring them closer!" barked the inspector. His men dragged the sacks forward. It was bloody and seemed to contain meat of some sort. "Open it!"

It was opened as dismembered parts fell alongside some clothing.

Karen stepped forward, brushing past the officers. Her eyes opened wide in horror as they fell on the parts as well as the clothing; the blood stained uniforms of her children. She slumped in a faint.

The inspector wasn't satisfied. He made for the huge stand:

"Don't go there," the woman who had brought them in said, "It is finished. Can't you see the children here?"

Whaaaaaaaam!

She fell to the floor before her brain registered what hit her as the swipe of a slap sent her way by the corporal beside her. The inspector walked around the stand and felt around it, for something.

There has to be a lever or secret knob, he thought to himself. *Aha!* His hand connected with it and he clicked the odd part up. A door opened and he walked into the room. There were at least thirty children in there, all unconscious on the floor without clothes.

"Jesus Christ!! Corporal, come here immediately! Radio medics, get an ambulance! Get people here! Jesus Christ! Ah! Am I talking to idiots? These children are alive! Someone get me the medics! NOW!"

NIGHT BLINK

The bullet whizzed past. It was so close she felt the heat. The target car was a distance away. They flew their best towards it, and shot back blindly trying to divert the attention of their assailants. It was not working. The darkness swallowed the shapes that approached them. The only clues they got of the enemy were the fires at the muzzles—the report from their guns.

Pow! Pow!! Pow!! Tratattatatattata! Pow! Pow!

There was no time to steady and aim. Suddenly the fires began to appear from a different direction.

"Hassan!" she shouted as her closest comrade fell to the ground. She bent to him and felt the heat again. She was in the air again firing back blindly. She cast a quick glance at the three men beside her. The fire from their muzzles showed their faces; grimly set. For a second she forgot the moment, the danger, and smiled. She was proud to be in their midst. Friends forever. She heard shouts of pain from the two different directions of the assailants and knew they had done some damage. It also brought her back to the moment.

"Yes!"

The opposing shots seemed to stop for a moment and they used the precious seconds to increase the distance and reach their vehicle. She quickly opened a door and jumped in. She turned the key in the ignition, just as two of the others reached. She noted that Kunle had the bag with him as he took the front passenger seat beside her.

"Drive!" Kunle shouted.

"Ibun is a few seconds away!"

Ibun dove in through the rear door, some bullets accompanying.

His instant lifeless body fell on Ida as the bullets tore through his entire frame.

"No!" Ida felt deep sorrow, intense anger, and in that second jumped out shooting in the direction of the opposing fire.

"Ida!"

But he was far past hearing in his raging charge towards the assailants.

She pushed the door open as Kunle's leg jammed the accelerator from his side. The dust flew as the car sped forth at full throttle. She fell back to the seat. She struggled up, turned to look behind them and saw Ida's body hit the ground. Tears filled her eyes as she turned to Kunle.

"We would have been killed too. Keep your mind on the road..." he said in a weary voice.

She was mute with shock. The car sped on passing a tee-junction. She felt numb all over. She could not believe that the people she had grown to love and cherish as friends for a long time could just fade away in the space of a few minutes. Lights appeared from behind.

"Shit!" Kunle shouted, "Drive faster!"

He got into the back seat and reloaded his gun, head down.

Pow! Pow! Pow! The three bullets shattered their rear glass. Kunle stuck his hand up and shot without aim.

"Arrrrrrrgghhhhhhhh!"

Screeeeeeeeeeeeeeeeeeeeeeech!

A loud shout of pain and some screeching assured him that his efforts had met with success. He raised his head:

"Yes!" The shout was for the victory of conquering the assailants. It was short-lived as he noticed another car coming in the distance:

"Damn! Drive faster!"

She drove on oblivious of Kunle. The car behind seemed to stop. Some minutes later, Kunle heaved a sigh of relief as he turned his attention to the front: "We seem to have lost them."

Yes, they had lost them. In the blink of one night, they had lost them all. She had seen Hassan falling to the ground. Hassan, the father of the recently born baby boy he had longed to have for years. Ibun fell unto Ida in blood. Ibun, whose mother kept calling him "My baby," though he was twenty-three years old. That sick mother in the village who would probably die of her strange ailment without the assistance of her two boys. There was the heroic Ida who would rather die with his brother in battle. She wondered what their mother would do. And Kunle...

"Ahhhhhhhh!"

She came back to as two shots found Kunle. She hit the brakes as he hit the back of her seat, his gun dropping out of his hand in the process.

"Kunle!" She reflexively carried the gun and moved to the back seat shooting at the vehicle Kunle had earlier seen.

Pow!! Pow!! Pow!! Pow!!

She fired some shots just as the car came to the side of theirs and hit bull's eye. She was hit in that instant too. Her breathing became hard, vision blurred. With her failing sight, she looked at the bag and wondered...

MUSIC FROM THE OTHER ROOM

I hear the sound come in. It is one I have heard before. I had danced several times to its many renditions. They hadn't been mine. They were those of my friends and recently, the very last of my sisters. It reminded me of all those days, when we were little. It was like the rain dropping. I have always been fascinated by that too—*tap, tap, tap*. It is a sound that has kept me company many times. Music now has come to be like that for me. Music playing, twisting through and through, they define it all: the sol-fa notes on and on punctuating heartbeats through pulsating notes of varying tempos. I am a music connoisseur and I can tell all the sounds individually. I can tell even where voices become mechanised or harmonised with some instrument or machine.

I am that good.

Music has come to define every life experience for me. It is and was always one song or the other—mostly beautiful tunes, especially those from the other sides, the other rooms. They were the blistering songs of the dance rooms where recklessness hit the floor as couples danced at first meets, the ease of casual relationships energising their bones in abandon. Many times, the music was the dance and the dance was the music. For some, it became more intimate. There grew the different types of music, mainly that of the ballroom, many times of two hearts flowing step by step in many styles—tangos and simple waltz, they were always perfect when it stayed two. Sometimes, it moved differently and ceased with the intrusion of one more. Yes, I knew all the songs and I knew the dances. I have been there. I had been there.

You made most of it. I remember your genesis. Of course, I can tell the future from sound. But let us not lose rhythm. You. Yes, you. Your voice was *surely* the last thing to hold me or anyone. Your behaviour was something out of some savage place. You were in every sense of the word, unbred—and I didn't think it would be through to all the meanings of the word. I had placed you in the composition where you belonged—a tuneless song. You were rough and all but it didn't mean you didn't have brains. You were one of those silently brilliant ones.

We had come to be acquaintances and I took it you weren't too bad a person. Rough and gruff but okay. I noticed the moves and started to think of a concert—that of a duo. It was the 12th of February, two days to the toast of Siamese heartbeats. The lonely winds were all that were going to play for me that time. I steeled myself to watch on as others waltzed their evenings away. Many friends had come to tell me about who their partner would be. I sighed. The classics came to my aid drifting me away. It took me by surprise then when you said those words, out of nowhere:

"What would you say if I asked you out?"

There was noise everywhere but I answered immediately without thinking it over: "Yes. Okay." In that second, I thought of how to change your chords and make you fall into tune. I looked at you in that second and discovered it would take so much work but I would try. In that very second, I thought all these and a new song started to play. It was one I had heard in the lives of many. It was finally going to be mine. Then, you blurted as immediate as my answer:

"I was joking."

The song went flat—cut. Reflex? I simply changed the song back to the one playing before. Silence screamed as everyone turned to look at us. A few turned away after a while, embarrassed on my behalf, perhaps. I ignored these people who heard you shatter the melody that had started building for me. Those who would see me in a whole new light of wrong. You couldn't have known at that time but I had built a concert in that second for you, the concert had started from the time we became acquaintances.

It really was reflex, as you pointed out later but you don't just cancel a concert in session, or one about to be started, one newly created—*ahh*! Whatever. You don't *just* do that and expect to have everything come back together in one breath! No.

Later, much later, you made more moves, becoming a far better musician than I ever thought. I smiled at the efforts but never let it get to me till the big bangs of graduation came our way. You had taught me in your earlier instant action that one had to be patient to let the other know the right sets of notes to make it work. In love, there was no one hit wonder. You had to take time. All the way up to the wider world, you never stopped. You kept practicing and it seemed the tunes kept getting better. The thrill finally hit the spot and I knew I could say 'No' no more. You had learnt through the plays, teases and all. Even in my refusals, you had located the strings to my heart and now knew the exact chords—the way to play the tunes that were truly mine...

Yet...

I hear the sound now. I close my eyes and let my cardiac drums play the beats to my heart. I hear the music from the other room—I have heard it several times. This time, it plays in this room. I open my eyes and you are standing there, standing here, staring at me, hands proffered up, knees to the ground...

SIMPLY MORTAL

He met Adoo long ago, a stunning beauty: petite but full in every other office. Hers was a chocolate dark skin that shone through any season; glistening and moist. She had the most beautiful set of legs seen anywhere, complemented by a full back and perfect waist. An ample bosom that showcased a full chest and an endearing heart followed up and ended in a most rounded ever smiling face that delighted the weariest of souls. She also had a heart of such endless depths to match. Yes, Adoo was all of this and so much more. He—Ngusha—was not the beast, either. Well, not in any deformity. He was a hunk with a height to compensate for hers, and strength to show for her every frailty. He shared her complete smile and perfect denture in a remarkable face that brought older and younger opposites to obeisance. They seemed to complete each other, as everyone said. Nature seemed to agree for a rough wind always seemed to mellow to a loving whisper at their sight. It seemed a union made in heaven, as indeed they made it.

"I have a weakness for women I can't fight," the baritone always whispered to her in tears that broke her to pieces. She detested the weakness and might have left but she had hers too; it made her stay. So, it kept on till a daughter came on, further cementing their relationship in a love that grew stronger with every breath inhaled. They were a perfect team and brought up the dear child in a most wonderful way. Adoo had an eye for helping the less privileged and did this to the detriment of her pockets such that the Director of Finance in the State that she was, she hardly had anything to boast of, except perfumes: she was a lover of perfumes. An engineer, his income came as the bread where hers could not reach due to charity.

One day, Adoo received a call; Ngusha was in the hospital. It was the first of several visits that confirmed him HIV positive. Several people urged her to leave. This surely was the time to leave. As a couple, they had both fought through several trials, including Ngusha's weakness for women, together. It probably was the cause of his current predicament. This was the biggest trial. In all, Adoo's weakness prevailed. She loved him more than ever but wouldn't let him touch her, couldn't. Then, he was in the hospital once more. This time it was serious and seemed the end. She was there every second of it. Adoo cried and begged God for a miracle:

"He was faithful to his drugs, Lord. If it be for my sake, let him rise. Please." She cried over and over again till her tears, it seemed, healed him. He smiled in his healing that morning as she awoke after a troubled sleep.

"Hello, Dear." The familiar baritone said as she cleared her eyes to his voice. It was a near instant recovery. They were excited as he was discharged. At her instant prompting, he shaved and refreshed. For once, Adoo went out of her way and got him a suit and the best perfume she could get. And truly, it was the best. She got herself a dress, then, went to the hairdresser's. That evening was the best of their lives. They went to a classic restaurant with their daughter and had a meal spiced up with a radiating love that sparked the whole atmosphere with a fragrance that their combined perfumes couldn't compete with. Later, as the smiling daughter slept, a father and mother's loving hands pulled over a duvet. For them, the night was far from over as life called to them. The record player went on forever as they danced, she always leading, in a destined full moon. It was never better. And when forever came to an end, they proceeded to their room. Adoo slowly undressed as Ngusha followed her step, just like in the dance. He kissed her passionately as they made love like never before. Exhausted, they spoke in words only two conjoined hearts could understand. In the moments between those and sweet sleep in each other, he apologized for every single wrong he had done. She had no time for such trivialities; her man was back.

It is said that the spirit spares the favoured and postpones that moment till a time when the other wouldn't know. So, it was that the spirit came in at that moment between twilight and dawn. He misjudged this time as she felt it at that precise moment. Two voices singing as one can never mistake the absence of the other. No different emotion came for the departed he. Love was all she had had. As such, Adoo could think of none else to accompany him on this most important journey. Then, she screamed as a hand went straight to her mouth; hers. Motherly instinct overcame the lover's anguish. She could not wake her daughter up. But she could do only as much. She sobbed bitterly as twin rivulets of anguish, steeped in love, coursed down her face and unto his. She looked on at him with the love of all the years, her only weakness. Ngusha had been prepared and she did not fear for his eternity. For the journey there, her tears and love, the greatest gift, sped him in the greatest of ease. But how could she know?

LUASHIE's DOCTRINE

At that time when it is too dark for a man to recognise his own body, Luashie's eyes opened of a will of their own. His body wanted more sleep so he willed his eyes shut. He turned in his bed, changing to a new position for added comfort. As he did so, his body brushed that of his wife. The sleep vanished and he shot out of bed. He threw on a pair of trousers and a tee-shirt. He looked around his rented one-bedroom apartment and not able to make anything out of the darkness, felt his way to the door. His leg connected with the arm of one of his sleeping children on the floor:

"*Eeissh,*" grumbled his victim but the next second, the same voice turned into a snore.

Luashie tiptoed more carefully, and once out, made his way to mass. He had formed this routine to excuse his being present at his wife's rising. During their 'honey' days, they had gone to church together, but the days of such cheap pretence were past. She was religious but didn't go to church much these days. Her sleep always won. This sometimes gave him an edge of victory over her.

He got to the church and was not shocked to discover he was the only one who had come in yet. He waited twenty minutes before the next person arrived. He wanted to greet the new entrant and make some small talk but his pre-mass etiquette dictated that he stay and meditate on the mass ahead. He sighed and continued his meditation and prayers. Mercifully, benediction was about to start.

It did, and shortly thereafter, mass was underway. Luashie kept his eyes out for the extraordinary. One didn't see it often here but it was always worth looking out for. This place wasn't like those churches where you didn't need to look out for the extraordinary; they brought it to you live—even if you were blind. Just two weeks ago, he had been pressurized by his friend, Ugbo, to attend one of such services. As usual, there were several 'miracles'. Ugbo had kept poking him at each miracle. Luashie's eyes bulged, his mouth open at it all. It seemed like a passage from the Bible: the lame started walking; the deaf started hearing; the dumb started speaking...

Finally, a blind man was brought to the pastor by one of the deacons. There was a short interview between the pastor and the blind man:

"My good man, what is your name and for how long have you been blind?"

"My name is Dotun Akirinde. Pastor, I was born blind. I have been blind since I was born. In fact, my parents who gave birth to me were also blind before they *delivered* me."

"The Lord shall do his miracles...!" exclaimed the pastor.

"Ameeeeeeen!" thundered the congregation.

The speaking in tongues started in earnest and the whole healing process began. Suddenly, 'the Lord did it!'

"Praise the Lord! Halleluiah!" the excited congregation shouted.

A piece of green cloth was brought in by a church attendant. Everyone, including Luashie, wondered what was going to happen next. The pastor showed the cloth to Dotun:

"Dotun, what colour is this cloth?" demanded the pastor.

"It is green!" shouted Dotun.

"Praise the Lord!"

Born blind indeed! Luashie left the church in that instant, wondering whether to laugh or be annoyed at the time he had wasted.

Give me that ol' time religion, Luashie whistled mentally as he thought of his mother church. It wasn't like there weren't miracles here anyway. The last one had been sensational. It had happened on one of those rare days he had missed morning mass. While he had not been there in person, he had heard the whole story firsthand from a reliable source—a church elder that saw everything from the front pew.

From the account of things, during consecration, a snake had appeared from nowhere and approached the altar. The catechist, who had been kneeling at the altar, was the first to notice the deadly creature. Apparently forgetting where he was, the catechist screamed in a ladylike voice and fled the church. The congregation must have been incredulous or something—the elder didn't say. The priest temporarily lost his stance but continued the ritual as the snake found its way to the altar, where it instantly got burnt in full view of all.

Luashie got to see the dead snake later that same day. It did not have any burn marks but rather what appeared to be stone cuts. All the same, having heard the story from the adamant church elder, who was he to argue the details?

This morning, mass went on without any incidence, even at consecration.

Luashie headed for the altar to receive communion. He knelt down to wait for his turn and noticed that the lady beside him had painted her lips thick as if she had used a paint brush instead of a lipstick. *Women and their palaver, which kind... oh!* It was getting to his turn. *Look at how Father put the communion. Chai, it is as if Father's hand is touching her mouth. Kai! Now, it is my turn. Father, Lord, cleanse me of every evil and renew me in you.*

"Body of Christ," the priest intoned.

"Amen." Luashie replied as he headed back to his seat, his eyes on the lady with the lipstick. He saw where Father had touched the lips. *Hmm! What is it with some of these ladies? If only I wasn't receiving communion now...* He concluded prayers and crossed himself. It was time for announcements and far quicker than he would have loved, mass was over. Luashie thought of the feeling of goodness he always had especially with the church's doctrines and smiled. There was no way he was ever going to *even* think about changing his faith. He dragged himself up, genuflected at the centre row, towards the cross, did the sign of the cross and left the church premises.

He could not go home immediately. Work usually started at thirty minutes past eight and there was no way he was going home now, at seven o'clock.

He got to Ugbo's shop. Their discussion was largely on sports and politics. It never got any better. After a while, Ugbo's wife called. She wanted him to do something for her within and he had to go. Women!

Luashie thought of the several places he could go to, and discovered there was none he could realistically head for. The road home seemed so far and yet, so close. He walked home slowly, as if intending to crush every single stone on the road. He got home and met his wife awake, and about. If she greeted him first, insults would follow accompanied with complaints and finally, requests. So, he was always fast enough to greet her first:

"Morning, Mama Junior." After greeting, he always tried sneaking to the backyard or anywhere else where he could claim busyness till his bath time. There were those rare good days when she would let him be. Today was not one of them.

"Baba Junior! You have come back from mass late again!"

She always wanted him coming straight to the house after mass. She didn't *even* like him saying *How did you wake up?* to anyone. *Such was her love.* But as usual, she had missed mass today. At such times, there was always an excuse to pacify her or some attack:

"Ah-ahn, Mama K, I told you to be coming with me to mass. But you love your sleep more than our Lord Jesus Christ! I have told you that to be counted among the faithful, you must go for mass every day and receive communion. When Father decides we should do novena like today, how will you know?"

It was always a good strike. At this, she would usually mellow and say something of an apology. Either that or she would be silent and wear a contrite face. She hated being hit; sleep was her weak point. He would come to her at such times, look her straight in the eyes, and tell her simply:

"Woman, change."

It was one of those moments that he lived for each day. The children would come out at this time, as they did now, and he would add, as he did now:

"Aôndo a yange kwagh u kunya. May the heavens forbid such a shameful thing." Then go in. On such mornings, there was usually no wahala from her; absolutely no trouble.

"Wait!"

What? He wondered, shocked.

She grabbed and pulled his shirt back toward her; "Where did you say you are coming from?"

"Straight from the church."

"Which church?"

"St. Thaddeus of course!"

There was a malicious glint in her eyes as she approached him.

"Kuma! Kuma! Kuma!" she thundered, "Get me a mirror. Now!"

The anger in the voice sent the boy running as if ten demons were after him. His mother's fury could be worse than them all combined. He appeared with the mirror in the second.

The neighbours gathered to watch the impending spectacle. This wasn't to be missed for anything. It was only comparable to the improving Nollywood soaps but this one was LIVE! Perhaps, some World Wrestling stunts would be added to the thrill!

"For the last time, Luashie, where did you go to after mass this morning?"

Luashie looked at his wife who stood a few inches above him in height. Her larger stature did not help issues. He swallowed: "Eh, I went to see Ugbo after mass."

"Are you telling me the truth?"

"Yes...Dear."

"Are you a homosexual?"

"I beg your pard—!!"

The mirror came to his face: Lipstick on his lips!

His preceding defence didn't help matters.

* * *

Why did the church rule out divorce? And if it wasn't for that stupid communion...

As Luashie counted the boxed ceiling of the hospital room where he lay admitted, he doubted his love for the church and her doctrines. He knew he wasn't going to be with the mother church too long.

A LUST INTERVENTION

*On a certain cold night, forces come to play and a man finds out he must
fight a certain craving for a warmth he desires.*

Tarlumun tried to pick out what it was about Amina that held
him most captive. It wasn't much of a successful exercise. Not
with her so close; not with her scent in his nose. Her eyes were
fixed on the portable DVD screen that he had given her the day before.
He was glad she loved it. Glad he could do something for her. He had
come to Mbanor where he had finished an assignment some two
months ago. It was during the assignment—the construction of a new
hospital, that he had met her.

"Have you eaten anything?" she asked, breaking into his thoughts.

"Eh—"

"You want to kill yourself?" She headed for the kitchen.

"No, you don't have to..." They both knew this was mere talk. He
had come to relish her meals. It was one of the things that had drawn
him to her. It was what had endeared her to him first. She had gone to
the site to inquire if she could get a contract to supply some building
materials. She had walked straight to him and stated her mission
without any fear or preamble, almost rudely. He did not have time for
such girls—he did not have time at all. He had told her that there was no
room for such and that she should not bother coming again. He was
sure he wouldn't see her again. He had a voice that could send a
platoon running. The hunger of the afternoon added a coarseness he
knew would chase a legion of demons away. He had forgotten about

her till the evening when she came with a flask of food. It was near perfect timing for he had planned to stay four more hours on the site. Still, he had to ask a few questions:

"What is this?"

"You sounded like someone who needs a meal at the end of each day."

Ignoring his instincts, he had smiled and eaten the food with relish. She became a near regular visitor to the site. It wasn't long before he became a regular visitor to her house.

"*Ohh!*"

Again, her voice brought him back to the present. The DVD battery had gone out. "And I don't know when this PHCN will bring light!" After a while, she added, "The room is stuffy, maybe we should go out for some air. I am taking your food out for you." They stepped out to the veranda and sat under the almond tree that stood in the middle of the compound. He wolfed down his meal. As she carried the plates back to the room, he took the opportunity to assess her figure or rather, her backside properly. The buttocks were round and big like two giant gourds; an alluring sight.

She returned from within shortly. He used the light of the full moon to look at her face as she spoke; the way her full pouting lips kept throwing one word after the other with swift grace left him thinking not of what she was saying but how those lips would taste. Her almond eyes shone brightly and almost seemed to be smiling. He took her hand in one of his and with the other, stroked her face gently. She continued talking as if she wasn't the one being stroked so. He tickled her in the ribs, the ear and she did same too. They giggled lightly. He started feeling the cold. Then, it was her buttocks he was feeling. He had several ideas... His instincts warned him. His ethics and faith shouted. He remembered his fiancée, Nnena, at home. Wouldn't it be a betrayal? Several thoughts came to his mind... He stood up and told her he was leaving. She objected and they played a bit more... Then, he stood up and headed for the main road. He knew he had to get a bike or taxi back home and fast. He was losing his strength, and resistance.

Nnena, the name kept jumping to his thoughts. A bike came at full speed. He tried flagging it down but she told him not to waste his time as the bike man wouldn't stop. He persisted and true to her words, the bike passed. His brows arched as he smiled:

"How did you know?"

"I feel," she answered.

"I feel too," he retorted lightly and moved to grab her in a bear hug. She was glowing.

"What *really* do you feel?"

"Warmth."

"Warmth?" she asked, sounding confused. But her eyes twinkled knowingly. "It is cold," she added.

He flagged down an oncoming vehicle and turned to her: "I mean you are warm, and open."

She was smiling.

He called his destination and the driver called an outrageous amount. He haggled the fare with the driver. There were hardly any passengers around. Having the premonition it might take some time to reach an agreement, the driver killed the engine to push for a proper bargain. He wasn't in a hurry. Amina tried to discourage Tarlumun's leaving. He tried to discourage himself too but felt a force pulling him into the vehicle. The name 'Nnena' played on in his heart. Between pleading with Amina that he had to leave and haggling further, his brain played 'to be' or 'not to be' games. The engine came alive; no time. He stepped away from the car and hugged her. She hugged tight, trying to draw him back.

"It seems you might be staying a while." She hugged him to her chest, throwing her arms around his neck. He felt the stiffness that her berries had come to be. He clung on to her till something deep shouted into his ears—Nnena! He pushed her and rushed after and into the car:

"Drive, fast!"

It was a cold night and he was going to regret not taking the extra meal but, it was worth it. As his body lashed him, his conscience patted him.

As the taillights of the car darkened away to the night, a demon whispered: "What happened? How could you let him go? We made everything perfect. All it took was for you to insist!"

"I tried. I used all the powers. I even put the final potent love powder in his meal today!"

"It is too bad. He is taking his prosperity and a lot more blessings that could easily have been yours—the merging of two into one. He could have been your slave. Too bad Amina. You know the repercussions of your failure, don't you?"

She shivered.

In a distant place: "Amen." Nnena said, crossing herself and concluding her intercessory prayer for Tarlumun.

FINDING NEW ROUTES

On this day, you decide to travel. It is one of those journeys to the far South. Everyone has been saying that the country is retrogressing. You were always on the defensive but as recent events begin to unfold, you have joined the centre, sitting on the fence. You keep a list of things you would use to defend the progress of the country. You drop your car at home. Why stress yourself when somebody can do the slave job for you? Then, there is the opportunity of meeting new people, who knows? You sacrifice your comfort for the beauty of a great tour. You get to the motor park and quickly board a vehicle going your way.

You look at your fellow passengers in the ash-interior seven-seater space bus. There is a slim woman with two children who are probably not more than eleven; there is a man with a fine face who you nearly envy till he greets you. Two prominent front teeth are missing. The remaining teeth tell tales of a long history of kola nut chewing. You don't care much for the remaining passengers. It doesn't take too long before the journey starts. You think of the age of the car and wonder how many hours you will take on the road.

To everyone's chagrin, you ask the driver to take his time:

"The main thing is to arrive alive, my guy."

You want to make ample use of the journey, take in the beauty and sights of everywhere. For today, you are a tourist. The driver sees a comrade in you and rewards you with a big smile. He is a young man with an old soul:

"Oga, na you be my guy!" He says and slaps your hand in salute. You hit it up and begin to talk. From foreign affairs to women affairs;

football to politics and matters of state, you chat on like soul mates. At some point, you have a disagreement that leads to an argument. The silence eats up the journey stretching it longer but you have the joys of scenery again: the plain lands of the North, camels, cows, nomads... You take it in all the way as you move southwards. The driver makes several stops and they seem to be the only annoying thing because all the passengers seem to want to buy one thing or the other at each stop. To make matters worse, the children begin to make so much noise. They bring different toys out of their bag and it begins to piss you off. But they are not done yet. They beg you to buy them *dis* or *dat* at different points. Their mother doesn't seem to mind as she smiles encouragingly at them. Soon, they are touching you:

"Uncle, what is your name?"

"Uncle, do you have children?"

"Uncle, why don't you have a big stomach like our Headmaster? Is it because you don't have money?"

You don't like their seeming *overt* familiarisation. Worse, you don't like their calling you 'Uncle'. Do you look like a sibling of either of their parents? You are ready to hold your peace till they decide to throw the biggest bomb:

"Your bald head is too shiny, Uncle..."

You are nauseated by them and admonish them differently. Finally, you bark at them:

"Back off! Rascals!"

That does the trick. They let you be. You smile.

After what is probably forever to everyone, the driver stops to correct a fault on the car. The tire needs to be replaced or something of the like. *Who cares?* You nearly ask as you smile but the hisses of your fellow passengers answer your unasked question. There seem to be a lot of appointments to be met. The children don't seem to care too and begin to carry some toys or something in a carton from the boot. You are grateful for a chance to stretch and explore a bit. Your bladder also signals a need for an urgent release.

"Five minutes!" The driver warns, but who says he is your father?

You know they can't leave without you. You walk a bit into a certain bush, led by a spirit you don't know. You see a rail line and decide to follow it. This is still in the all bushy place. You are following the rail line now. You thought they were extinct but remember that some trains still exist and might ply this route. Relishing the days of the train, you walk towards it. Memories chug down your brain in rumbles, bustles and loud whistles. You remember the few kobos and ease of transport that was always a new adventure each time you climbed a carriage. There were the tears of departing in anxiety, the adventure of the trip and yes, the smiles and laughter at return. Each journey always had its tale. The sounds fade out and silence echoes current reality; the only way to travel here is by road or air; the common man's choice limited to the former. You sigh wondering when, if ever, the rail will come back to full use. You hope that the Governor who is implementing it in his state will take it all the way. *The entire load carried in big vehicles that destroy the roads so painfully constructed can easily be carried through this means*, you think to yourself. You make a note to write an article on this when you get to civilization.

Then, you notice it as your jaw drops; a shrine sitting on the rail! Incredible! You rub your eyes to be sure this is not a painting or movie set. It is real. Your lower arm pushes your jaw as your mouth closes, shutting out an incoming fly. You might have done something, but you dash back to the car robotically to get your camera. You get it and rush back to your scoop. Just as you steady your camera, a hand taps you:

"What are you trying to do?"

You turn and look at him, a tall black man dressed in a suit. What kind of question is that? You are about to ask but something holds your tongue.

"What are you trying to do?" he repeats.

You are pissed at his audacity and think of what to say to him when he speaks again, "You dare not."

This is certainly out of hand and your mouth decides it has had enough. At this, he opens his suit for you to see the inside, two beautiful black shiny PISTOLS! In that instant, you remember several stories of ordinary and usually innocent people who were found with sophisticated guns, who wanted to fire a security officer but were shot first. Who would believe your story? You feel liquid stream down your legs and you know this isn't sweat.

"Aminu! Come, *e be laik say we don get sacrifice!*"

"Jesus!" You hear yourself exclaim.

"*Sharap!*" the man barks as he brings out a pistol. You are already thinking of all the things you have not accomplished in your life and you feel your bowels getting heavier still. "Aminu!" the man shouts again as he turns to look in the direction that his mate should be coming from. You both hear some loud sounds not too far away. They are probably gunshots. The man ducks as the sounds come again.

Are they coming closer? You wonder. In the confusion the sounds create, you take to your heels and let adrenaline do its magic.

"*Kai!* Stop or I shoot!" you hear the man's voice boom. You can almost hear his legs in flight after you when you hear another voice shout:

"*E fit be say im get pipu fo dia...!*"

You don't hear the rest and you don't care much for it. You seem to hear more feet following you. You don't look back but put your whole spirit into the race for the car. Your head doesn't recognise the direction of your feet and the only thing on your mind is 'LIFE!' You get to the road and discover the car moving already. You shout with all the life you can breathe into words:

"WAIT!"

The driver pushes open your door as you reach the car and you almost fly into the car to the astonishment of the other passengers.

"*Na wetin?*" They all seem to ask at the same time, wondering what is wrong with you.

"Drive!" You manage to say and add "Fast!" between quick breaths as you look back every five or so seconds. The car seems to be snailing to you. No speed seems fast enough though the dashboard reveals the driver's speed as 150mph. It is only after a long distance and a million turns back to be sure you are safe, that you sigh in relief. By this time several theories have emerged of what you saw from the different passengers: 'Mami wata' 'Snake' 'Lion' 'Spirit'...

One of the boys fiddles with a small box, then flings something out of the window—a firecracker—and you hear a very loud noise. You discover that this is what you probably heard in the bush. You sigh in relief and turn to the boys, a huge smile playing at your lips:

"My name is Uncle Pringkwap. Do you mind having a treat on me when we reach where we are going?"

TRAILS TO THE TALE

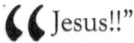"Jesus!!"

The news had just reached them. Nineteen of their colleagues had been murdered. The bodies had been found. As if the phone was waiting, it rang at that moment. It was Fatima, Santim's wife. She had kept calling since the news of the 'disappearance' of the nineteen soldiers had leaked. Santim, Mgbo's cousin, was one of them. He couldn't bring himself to answer immediately. After two more rings, he pressed the answer key:

"He is meant to be on vacation," she said, fear quavering those words that echoed a million times more in her quiet voice; "Please, tell me he is not one of them?"

"Fatima, I ... I... I am sorry." Mgbo heard a thud. "Hello... Hello... Hello! Are you there? Hello!"

He went to their house at the close of day, composing himself. Contorted faces decorated the essence of the crowd that stood in front of the house; several shook their heads sadly. Mgbo asked what the problem was and found out Fatima had collapsed to her death earlier on; the thud he had heard during the call. He thought of the six children, complete orphans.

"By God, those Tiv assholes will pay for this!" he swore to himself.

Much later, Modatus, Mgbo's friend, tried to console him. It was beyond simple grief but how could Modatus understand? How could he understand the pain of Santim and Fatima? What was the point of explaining shared histories, pasts, joys, fun and even troubles never to be got or reminisced over again? Mgbo wished that something like Odi would come to bear again. He headed home, knelt down and for the first time in many years, prayed: that the order would come for Gbeji and that it would come to their camp.

The order came two days later. Mgbo smiled as he packed his things to get prepared for them. If Naijaria thought they had seen anything in the Odi massacres, they were in for a shock. Mgbo had missed that one and thought the massacres were wrong. *This one has a righteous backing*, he thought. After all, God had answered his prayers.

*

Modatus was one of the soldiers who had been deployed to Gbeji. He did not understand why they had been called over but was glad that this was a peacekeeping mission. In another life, he might have been angered at the request. However this was a year after Odi. It all came alive to him once more. Certain police officers had been killed in Odi and the President had ordered them to go and quell the situation. He closed his eyes as the gore of innocent blood hit him in the face. Mgbo hadn't really recovered from Odi. It felt like Abel's blood still cried against him.

It was the third day since they had come around. There was going to be a meeting later in the day at the market square and in other areas. For the first time, the army was going to be different—they were truly going to keep the peace and save the Tiv from their neighbours—the Kumbus—who, intelligence report had suggested, would make a move to annihilate them. He smiled. Well, they were here on a peacekeeping mission and he was prepared to give it his all. This was his atonement for all he had done in Odi. He would protect the people despite the death of his colleagues. It was painful but even as a professional soldier, he knew that some blood didn't answer the call of blood.

* *

By 10:00 AM, the garage square was filled to capacity. The garage was in reality, a commercial motor park. At least, that was its primary function. It had served as a meeting point of sorts and several village disputes had seen their end there. Time had raced past fast and a lot of people shifted restlessly as they waited. They might have left but there was an important matter whose horns had to be cut. The elders who had been in support of a resolution through dialogue had done a good job of convincing people to attend. It seemed the whole town was in attendance:

"Violence is not the answer," an elder had preached to the impromptu gathering of youth the day before. "The soldiers have called all of us to a meeting so as to resolve all issues. As you all know, the people had posed in military uniforms and caused destruction to our parts. They killed some people too. We asked the soldiers who said they know nothing of it. We, the elders, cautioned patience and forgiveness. You children with the hot blood of aggression we are known for, decided to avenge the pride of our village. The rapes and ravages had gone too far. The Kumbu people had indeed gone too far." At this, he paused for effect, heads nodded him on.

"Still, our grey hair has taught us that this isn't the answer. We have seen the Biafran war, the Liberian war and know that though both are holes, the mouth is a far better talker than the muzzle. You thought with your hands instead of brains, as youth is wont to. Six of the men in military uniform were seen in a part of the village. Whether they were our previous visitors, we cannot say. You caught them and brought them to our headquarters, Gbaagol. You stripped them and humiliated them publicly. In a 'feat' not known to our parts, you cut them apart, organ by organ before burning them. The smoke went to the skies and spread all the way to the barracks where their absence was noted. They say there were nineteen but what do we say?

How do we deny? Do we say to the father of the impregnated girl that we had sex with the girl but are innocent because we used a condom?"

A resounding 'No!' and chuckles had greeted this. The talking elder, Igba, continued:

"The soldiers came and picked the offenders. They wanted to crush us but we, the elders, intervened and reached a truce. They said they will meet with us at the garage by ten a.m. for a meeting of the two sides. We suggested the town hall for its symbolic stance but they insisted they wanted a wider place. They insisted. Let us thank Aôndo this is a democratic country now. Only God knows what would have happened if they had the right to instant might as then. Still, they are the holders of our guns and we have to cooperate with them. Remember 'mistaken fire'?"

They laughed at this. Mistaken fire was another name for 'accidental discharge,' a situation where people of the armed forces shot someone and claim it is a mistake; an accident.

"Everyone is meant to be there. The focus is men but still; bring your wives and children so they can learn. The women are the teachers: When they watch such things, they usually learn how to instruct the little ones in ways that they should grow."

That was yesterday. Today, Igba would have been delighted at the impact of his words that had brought so many. It did not matter that the farmers were not in season and that the garage was in the market which enabled people to excuse their wares in a few minutes. It did not matter that a lot of people were just plain bored and needed some entertainment which they believed the public redress would bring. It also did not matter that a few people were afraid of what would befall their village if the soldiers met an empty garage. What mattered was that an elder had spoken and people had decided to hearken to his words. The old order of the wisdom of the elders was coming back. Technology and civilisation had surely not taken everything after all. These were people who loved peace.

They all came, noting the soldiers at the gates, sentries. The soldiers advised that the women and children leave but the elders *insisted* that they stay so as to learn. They noted the full combat gear of the soldiers too. Well, who knew what they wanted to demonstrate to the people? The women tried their best at controlling the children who kept running about. Time dragged as everyone waited for the Army Chief—the Big Oga—who had promised to come. The elders seated regally in the centre of the garage began to fan furiously, ceremony lost. Of all days, the sun had decided to up its heat notches today. The elders began to question the wisdom in wearing their traditional uniforms of thick materials of black and white stripes. On cold days, it was a pleasure as it kept them warm. On this day though, the uniforms served as punishment. The others who custom didn't force to dress as such smiled. They were happy not to be that old, for once.

* * *

So far, he had assured the people around of the peacekeeping stance. The villagers were naturally scared and apprehensive of all the heavy artillery—from tanks to sophisticated weapons—that had been brought.

Then, the order came from above: Gbeji was to be brought down, like Odi.

Modatus bit his lip as rivulets coursed down his face. "*Damn!* I hate the army!" he blurted.

"Hate the heat? *Comot* from the bloody kitchen *jare!!*"

There was a deadly glint in Mgbo's eyes. He seemed to be high on some drugs, maybe marijuana or something. *Yes*, Modatus thought, *I definitely need to have some of that. Damn!*

* * * *

At 12:30p.m., it was getting obvious that the Big Oga was not coming. The people, who were highly uncomfortable as it was, began to disperse. Some attempted to leave the garage and noticed only then that the main gates were barred. This was puzzling. Then,

Peeeeeeeeeeeeeeeeeeeeeeeep!!!

A shrill whistle rang freezing all civilian movement in shock. Not so for the military personnel whose lightening precision held everyone more shocked. Every exit had been blocked. The ring around the gathered people was noticed in that instant. Ghost feet might have been heard in the descended hush; then the cry of a baby tore it. It seemed the agreed sign, for the numerous muzzles began to spit fire. Commotion broke as legs found strides. Bullets pursued each cutting runs to falls.

The old tried to muster energy lost in youth to pull tables or whatever to take cover. It was useless for the space was open, the shooters experts. The choice hadn't been a mistake. Slowly, the pile rose up till not a single person was left standing.

The khaki wearers jumped down from their various vantage points as their leader led the way. He kicked over the bodies to be sure. The babies lay with bullets designing their cherubic features, torn. There were women with red all over reminiscent of pregnancies and menstruation. Pregnant women lay dead with bullet riddled stomachs. Thus lay unborn babies tasting the realities of a harsh existence before being born into a world they would never see. Able bodied men were left useless by metals, smaller than the finger of a baby. On the ground also were big bellied elders whose wisdom the bluntness of bullets had wiped out in brains splattered all over.

Soldiers pushed bodies aside to be sure of annihilation. A soldier saw a man breathing heavily, groaning. The heavily black and white striped cloth didn't help much.

"Wh– wh- wh - wh…" he struggled to say something, a question perhaps. A bullet to the forehead completed it for Chief Igba.

"*Anofia!*" the Sergeant shouted as he sent a ball of spittle at Chief Igba as if to end his sentence. The word, translated, meant 'wild animal.' "Next time, they will know who to mess with. Boys! Let's go!"

Adrenaline's Magic

His legs, as they say, touched his head in full flight. Bem wished his legs could go farther than his skull. The Malo guys were fast on his trail and he had to put some distance between them. At this rate he could have won any Olympic race. He leapt over an upturned drum. He reeked of fuel. In a different situation, someone seeing him might have thought it was the fuel that gave him speed. *So much for thinking only vehicles used it!* Despite his full adrenaline, drench and fear, a flash smile appeared:

Fuel for his speed. Only vehicles, abi? He looked to his eyes' limit and noticed a deserted road. When would he get to anyone? He looked to the trees and buildings. Even they looked menacing and so, he continued farther. He looked forward and backward several times in order to be sure no one was following him. Though they were a distance from his sight he could hear their voices. A few days ago, his friend had told him the story of a man whose buttocks had been slashed in full flight. It had seemed funny, then. A man in full flight, then, *swoosh!* No butt again. His reaction to the gist had been instant:

"Ha! Ha! Ha! Ha! Ha! Ha! Ha! O boy, you *sabi* lie o!" In the battlefield, the story seemed like it could be his at any moment.

But which evil spirit had prompted me out? A million curses and more! If he had known he would meet those Malo guys... He had run, actually walked into them:

"Stop there!" the obvious leader had commanded, "Where *I* dey go?" he asked, his way of demanding where Bem was heading to. Fear had seized the laughter that would have greeted this blunder.

"I dey try reach school"

It was either the leader didn't hear him or thought Bem meant he was a staff member in school. The order was given and *tua*!! A slap cut across his face.

"*Aôndo*!!" he cried, calling God.

Gbuum!! *Kpaa*!! *Gbua*!! The several slaps, blows and other forms of brutality not recorded in any written vocabulary kept flying at Bem:

"I am a student! I am a student! Wan ye makanta! Eh!! *Yaron makaranta*!! *Dalibi*... I be student! I be... *arrrghh*! *Ayoooo*!! Aôndo!!" English, Tiv, Hausa, Pidgin and the unmistakable language of pain! He kept the varying chant which acted as some sort of background music to the men who increased their pace with each 'drop.'

"*M kpe ve o*!! I am dead! *Na mutu*! I be student na!!" He kept on crying as he continued in cycles, in words and movement while the Malos changed their brutalities. A big plank with nails on it appeared from nowhere. A cutlass followed in quick succession. The wielders were swift and seemed professionals. From accounts, it took three seconds. Two in the air and *swoosh*!! You were... Bem knew this and despite his pains now, prayed all the recitals he had learnt from his youth. Up and...

"Stop!" It was the leader. Bem heaved a sigh of relief.

"I promise to go to mass each day and never miss tithes and offertory. No more girls and..." He kept making more fear instant promises.

"Student!" Finally, it seemed someone had heard him. The leader looked at him and smiled.

"Yes," Bem responded with blood stained teeth. The leader said something Bem didn't understand. But then, the message wasn't his. He caught a breather at his attackers' break. He sat down on the ground, still continuing his promises. *Voop*!! A tire fell on his neck. The men shouted in glee as fuel was poured on him. Such a show was definitely to be enjoyed. The plan had been to weaken him, then in that state, burn him.

Thump! Someone fell with a loud crash and with it, the attention of the remaining eight. The jet took off without any ceremony and shot into full flight. Adrenaline was an amazing human component and at this second, Bem praised God for it. He now knew why their goat had disappeared last Christmas after seeing a knife. Danger sure made man and other animals alike.

"Heyaaaa!" "Ayaaaaa!" Bem heard the sounds in the distance as his thoughts darted back to the present. He ran with renewed vigour and 'blissfully' into the arms of another Malo group.

"Stop here!" He tried to run but at that instant, a weakened and fearful heart coupled with tired legs, emptied him of all his strength, and adrenaline. The group seized him as he readied himself for death, the promises still on the tongue of his heart.

"I will never cheat in my exams...nor lie, ever... I will love you more..."

"Release him!" the leader barked as Bem fell to the floor. His tone became softer "You are a student, *ko*?" Bem affirmed with a nod of the head. "In that case, I would let..."

The first attacking group arrived at this moment, and asked for their prisoner. There were some negotiations and the second leader with a resigned look on his face gave way to the verdict. It was three seconds. The cutlass was raised. With tears and a combination of sweat, fuel and urine, Bem perfectly understood the smell of a he-goat, especially a dead one. He passed out.

EYES OF THE ROAD

The rain hammered all as it lashed out at those below. There were puddles everywhere. The gutters were filled with filth; empty satchets of water, biscuit wraps, chewed corn cobs, polythene bags and much more. However, there was a journey to be undertaken. Destination was the target and no flood, or anything else would stop the objective. After what seemed like a millennium of minutes stemming into hours, a bus drove into the park. All the waiting passengers ran into it. It was a transport company's park. It turned out this bus was not a registered bus of the company. It appeared to have been picked from a private commercial driver to compensate for the absence of the registered vehicles. Not long after this, a registered vehicle came. An official tout or *agbero*, as they were called here, for this park ordered all the passengers to come down and enter the more recent entrant. A quick comparison between the two vehicles found the passengers protesting and staying put. This infuriated the tout who threatened hell. Not even his sweaty dark face laced with a deep gash, a million pimples and an ugly frown were enough to change the stance of the passengers. No effect so he resorted to challenging the driver. The driver quietly called him and told him to transfer the luggage in the boot. The tout knew this wasn't a charitable deed and instantly calmed down, as he smiled:

"Well, I forgive you because you get sense small. But na only for today."

He collected the money for his job which was more than the driver of the other bus would have paid him and bid the fine vehicle farewell.

I smiled in satisfaction. I hated travelling in the rain. However, I preferred it to standing in the rain. I picked a scarf from my bag and tied my head to pray. A lady once told me the story of a girl and her mother. The girl was going for a picnic with her friends. Her mother bade her farewell and prayed God go with her. The girl replied her mother, "There is no space in the car for God. However, if God wants to come *by force*, he can come in the boot." She set out for the trip with her friends, and had a ghastly accident. The car was totally smashed and squeezed. Miraculously though, nothing happened to the boot. Every single item in the boot, including raw eggs in crates, remained unbroken and intact. The story was enough to remind me of prayer each journey. And of course, with the state of bad roads, one had to pray as a matter of 'can't help'. One had to either pray for journey mercies or for the grace not to see any accident or gory sight on the road. I crossed myself and picked the former as my intention.

This bus was spacious and the luxury, quite uncommon, became my ice breaker with my neighbour friend. We laughed.

"We will arrive in four hours," he said. Four hours was the standard length of the journey.

Assessing the vehicle again, I replied:

"No. Definitely three hours or three and a half at most."

An hour later, we had not reached the boundary of the next state. This was a distance from Makurdi that took only thirty minutes. We were going below snail speed. Cars passed; buses, bikes and even trucks! Some passengers had the temptation of dropping and jogging ahead of the bus. I had a feeling they would arrive our destination before this bus. We moved as more vehicles overtook. Everyone insulted the driver. The vehicle we left in the park, that hadn't even been boarded then, soon overtook us. Storms of insults came pouring on the driver from all corners. Shouts of "Idiot!" "Which kain driver be dis?" "Learner!" "Mr. No License" "Chief Nonsense" "Oga Go-Slow" to mention the polite ones, rent the air. Appointments had to be met! The driver noticed the tension.

"Abeg! Abeg!" He tried to seek the passengers' understanding in words drowned by a general uproar.

An angry hand struck the driver. It was now leaving the realm of words. People began to stretch closer to express their minds with their hands. Just lightly at first. Then a man with a monstrously big hand removed a weapon or something to threaten the driver. Just as he lifted it, the driver braked and the noise changed from insults to exclamations:

"Jesus!"

I saw two people in the bush; legs spread lying on the grass. Like a bolt it dawned on me, a fresh accident. The car that had just overtaken us! A head-on collision and death on the spot for twelve! Twelve people in all—mostly students, as uniforms proclaimed. We stopped. Curiosity reigned—not for me and two other women. Next, prayers and in abundance, tears. The driver was the first to return. Wet eyed, he began to speak in a shaky voice:

"This rain and bad roads! Kai! Kai! That's why I have been driving slow. I have seen blood on this road o! Kai! I have seen bloooood ooo... Oh God! Kai!"

"Take heart Oga Driver. You are a man. Be strong."

He did his best **to** compose himself and tooted his horn. It was the sign to tell the passengers that the time for the side show was over; time to go. Slowly, the bus filled back.

As the driver drove, silence and gratitude reigned; nothing more.

SMILES, SIGHS AND GROANS

He put his head in his hands. It was one of those days. He had to get his big sister, Karuna, a present. He definitely had to. He put his hand in the pocket of his pants. There was some money there. He smiled, then groaned as he glanced at his phone. It was his secretary:

"Yes?"

"Sir, the artist is on the way for his money. I need to get it from you before he arrives. I am on my way."

Sigh. "Okay."

He counted the money out of what he had found. There was barely Five Thousand Naira left. The various obligations flooded into his mind: this debt, that debt, this service, that payment; the carpenter working on the office shelves. Ah! What could he do? His secretary was soon in his house. He gave her the money for the carpenter and also, the artist. The designs and settings for the new book project were telling on him. He wondered why he made such a move. Ah! How many people read books these days?

He picked up his phone to call Karuna but changed his mind almost immediately. Not for the first time in his thirty years, Vasega was at a loss of what to do next. He scratched his head once more and decided that a note would be better. He couldn't bear to let Karuna hear his voice. He sent her a couple of text messages. Then he sent a different set to Shai, her husband. After all, it was their birthday. The 'Delivered' return message from his network provider assured him the messages had gone through. He logged in to Facebook and discovered that his younger sister had beat him to it. She had sent a birthday wish.

Sonia had been her witty self wishing their big sister the best. She had added a message for Shai. The couple had replied and Vasega could almost hear their laughter. Writing anything now would be to ape what Sonia had done. It would seem that she had taken the shine. He sighed once more. If only Sonia hadn't tagged him, perhaps he wouldn't have seen it. But well, he had sent Karuna text messages. He smiled. But she hadn't replied, was she mad at him? What of her husband? He remembered at that moment that his last exchange with them hadn't ended on a good note. Were they still pissed at him? Sigh.

He stepped out to his day, hoping to receive a miracle. He didn't find the needed miracle. He wondered if the parcel he had sent previously would get to them in time. If only he had sent it earlier, it might have been the perfect gift. He was sure that his poems would have been just the thing for her. She had been asking for them for a long time. It was a comfort to know the book was on its way. He smiled as he thought of what he had inscribed in the book. Again, his smile disappeared. He couldn't really remember what he had written in the book. He knew it had come from his heart though, and that each word written had carried a prayer of gratitude, love and the very best wishes for Karuna, who had come to be like a mother to him; although their mother was still alive. Thoughts of his mother came to him. Age wasn't smiling on her but she worked on with the strength of ten horses meeting every need of her seven children. Even with the independence of her children, she stood for them, aiding their every project, meeting their every need from the emotional to financial. Tears slowly came to Vasega's eyes as he thought of them all, his sisters and his mother; such amazing women. He cleaned his dry cheek and discovered the tears had only been thought. The strength of their mother had been passed to Karuna. She had seven children too and was twice the support of their mother to her family and siblings. She had stood for Vasega many times and it was for this reason that he decided to do something for her this year no matter what.

It was dusk as he arrived home. He picked the new book and looked at the poems within. There was one by a friend of his, "God bless on another day." He smiled as he read the lines again. His friend had told him it was an extempore poem written for some of his sisters—Karuna and Sonia's names—had appeared there. Extempore indeed. He mentally dedicated the poem to his sisters, too it wasn't only that fellow who had sisters! He felt lame though. Why use another person's poem when he could write one better. What did poetry take? Wasn't it just an expression of one's innermost feelings? Pbtttt! The ink of his thoughts flowed extempore too:

For the many years you came by
You reduced the length of a sigh
The sun shines but sometimes the cloud covers it
You are the line that is on every cloud knit

Words never might paint the length
Of love that our hearts measure out
But feel the power of its looming strength
The passion would cure your every doubt...

He wondered if she would like it. His phone rang. It was an important client who on occasion had stayed on the line for hours.

"Hello," Vasega said, talking into the phone. "Can you call back please? I am in the middle of twenty-four herculean labours plus one."

"It is important," the client replied, "I give you ten minutes or I will take the job to Apollo."

The line didn't go dead; the client was going to wait for those minutes. Well, ten minutes was good enough time. Clear the writing debt and get back to the client. Simple. He dropped the active phone on a stool and felt his pocket for his other phone. He brought out his pen and wrote a letter:

Dearest sis,

You might have left our lands long but the stars, I know, shine down there like they shine here. The moon might come out a bit late but it would still be the same one that we pursued across surfaces on many watered plains. I feel the wrinkles coming but smoothen them and let the play of the day continue to colour your every moment. This, I know, would rid you of every torment. It might be night here but day still tickles you there – though I can guess that even on your day, you would be more servant than served...

Dance with Shai, sis, enjoy the essence of that love that drove you wild. Look at the beauty of your several children, of our siblings and drink of the thoughts of us on this side. We might not send you all we wish but know, that even as we force words to flow, words that our feelings hardly show, you occupy a place that you might never know...

If I could ask for another sis, I would probably ask for one closer (laughs)... There might be many that life has blessed us with but you are one that remains a light none can dare compare to shine with...

Happy Birthday sis.

Your brother, Vasega...

He dropped his pen and stepped out. He looked to the skies. He noticed Orion's belt. It held a promise to the traveller:

"Keep her safe," Vasega whispered. "Keep her safe."

As he thought of Shai holding her in his usual possessive way, Vasega wondered if his prayer was to the stars, the heavens, Aôndo or to Shai. Maybe, all of them. He still looked at the stars as if expecting a sign. At that moment, a shooting star shot past. He made the sign of the cross and prayed for everyone else in his life. He thought of his sister Sonia and wondered whether to call her or not. He brought his phone out and discovered he had a message: the couple had replied him earlier: We will celebrate for you. Shai had said. Sonia's message read: Turkey and chicken. Thanks Vasega. I'm happy today for life and grace. You good? Just like her to check on him at all times. Vasega also had a missed call! Ouch! He had to call another lovely lady too. He shifted his worries aside with a mental wave and for the first time in his day, smiled fully. His sister would feel his heart's wish. Then he remembered: he had kept an important client on the line. That was thirty minutes earlier! Groan!

GARAGE BLUES

The day was extremely hot as was usual in Belye. I went to the garage to resume duty. I was hungry but who cared? I had to go to my job. Wow! Sometimes I wondered if my degree was worth it after all; after spending five academic years that were equivalent to ten years in the regular strike written dates of the Naijarian calendar... So high were my hopes then. A degree earned and the crippling hands of suffering would melt to let my wings fly to heights unknown. Ten harrowing years of headaches and five years of academic frustrations! Four specified and mandatory years for my course and an extra *jara* dashed by my lecturers–*haba*! What had they called it then? Yes, spill over, that was it. I had spent a lot of money on that course. Forget my school fees; forget all the dues and the various levies imposed on us. Forget the money for all those compulsory hand-outs, even though they had been banned. Did I just say hand-outs? Forgive me, I meant lecture notes. Strangely, they look, feel and are exactly like the hand-outs and what is more, people still buy them. Baptism was always a quick route and easy resort in this country. It reminds one of the famous story of the Reverend Father who caught his butler eating meat on Good Friday. The Priest asked his *boy* why he was eating meat on that day .

"It is fish," the accused quickly defended.

"Are you trying to say that I am blind?"

"No, Father. You see, the time *wey* I came here, they *bin de* call me Obinna. You pour water for my head and I turn to John. *Na* so me *maself*, I pour soup on top the meat head change am to fish."

Oh yes, and so goes the story of the lecture notes. But like I said, let us forget my finances. Let us also forget the *suffer-head* and midnight oil burnt to pass papers and get marks which scarcely came.

I finally found my way out of school with a gentleman's degree; a *two-two* or second class lower. I was excited because as I said before, it was the beginning of a hope where I would reach beyond the stars.

I had my compulsory one year national youth service experience as a teacher in Bantaje, a village in a remote corner of the country. I taught English and Literature in a community secondary school where most of my students didn't know how to speak English. On the bright side, I learnt a bit of the more prevalent Hausa of the community. Truth be told, the task of tutoring those million classes were a headache but I found inspiration by the river in the community, writing once in a while and soon the year passed by. Armed with a discharge certificate, I stormed the labour market.

What boundless opportunities awaited me over there, wow! It was smiles all through for me. I guess one could see my 'ear to ear'. The general saying I got accustomed to soon enough was; "In Naijaria, everyone is a graduate". Others were less polite and told me: "Degrees are like arses here, man. Everyone has one." It spelt a big "*Notin' for you!*" That pointed out to me that the whole cramming and learning just to pass in the university was for nothing. Memories of those mosquito-dominated 'till-day-break' readings didn't make sense any more. Too harsh but *mehn*, the temptation to turn to crime was high. A few people suggested full time crime to me: politics or the gun. But *haba*, a man with a heart wouldn't put his leg in that kind of dirty water. Truly, certain roads carried thorns too thick—in patience, thoughts and conscience. God pass devil!

Oh well, I thank the Almighty for my upbringing. Growing in Warri, the most notorious acclaimed *agbero* town of my country has taught me a lot. The street gospel has blessed me. I am a worthy ambassador of Warri so I decided to become self employed. This did not come spontaneously though. No, did it? If you think it did, you are wrong. Now, various options of clawing funds together played ping-pong in my head as I sought to enrol for my Master's degree programme. I had the conviction this one would be less common than the arse and thus get me something to hold my body together. In the process of my clawing, I chanced upon a friend who had a Master's degree and yet was a commercial motorcycle rider, an *okada* man. I was shocked, thinking that the sad plight of joblessness was only for the mere degree graduates like me. He gave me his version of this 'national anthem'. He did some preaching and I was changed. I saw the gains of self employment and that is where I am now—a conductor, a bus conductor in Belye.

*

Hunger changes even the best of us. Now, who will blame the prodigal son for wanting to eat pig food? But work calls above the stomach now. Presently, the bus is filled. The usual people and types; the same expressions and talks, only some different faces carry them today. It is so each time. One woman however catches my attention. She is Fulani and has a tin with her. I wonder what might be inside. The Fulani (their women at least) are always with cow milk or *nono* as they call it. For sure, I know that tin contains *nono*. To think that I have not eaten since yesterday... it is going to be an hour's journey so there will be enough time.

As if I knew it, the Fulani woman's face looks sickened. I guess it is the journey. Most of them get sick after we drive a while. She still holds unto the tin but I must take my focus from her lest she becomes suspicious. She is however soon asleep. All the passengers seem to be the 'I don't care' sort, so I quietly carry the tin. No one is *even* giving me any attention. I open the lid quietly and soon the contents go down my throat in one looong greedy gulp: *uuulp!* I lick my tongue, strange taste but well, it is all yuckishly good.

The journey ends soon, money is collected. As the Fulani woman gets ready to alight, she notices that her special tin is missing. There is worry written on her face or is it *concern*?

"*Wai ya doka rago na?*" Probably, "Who took my tin?"

"*Ni ne na doka. Na sha nonon ki.*" I know a bit of Hausa too and smilingly confess my crime in a little charged voice to cover the deep shame of my heart. Someone notes I am rude and taking advantage of the old woman. The lady does not seem to note my rudeness and in a very small voice says something close to:

"*Aya, da na! Abunde ka sha ba nono ba ne–amei na ne!*" My face goes pale as all smiles leave my being. In her simple terms: "*Oh my son. What you drank was not nono–it was my vomit!*"

Belye!!

A TALE OF ANOTHER'S CRIME

There were never two men
To claim my prize
One man...

He found himself in a white singlet and brown towel. There were people all around drinking. He was in a drinking hut? How had he got there? He heard a scream from the hospital across the road and ran towards its direction. He saw Dedoo. In the few seconds, he noticed that the worry lines on her face had grown longer and far deeper;

"Why are you not in there?" he breathlessly asked.

"Don't worry. She doesn't need me." There was a mixture of bitterness and sadness in her voice... "She—"

He hardly heard the last words as he dashed into the compound. He searched everywhere for the screamer, Adamma. He saw a group of his friends in the courtyard that divided the big hut from the other smaller one where the main business took place. He seized one of them by the arm:

"Where is Adamma?" They all pointed in the direction of the smaller hut. He let the man go as his heart rose in beat and speed. *She had been taken to the smaller hut?* He feared the worst as he rushed in the direction they had pointed. She was not in there. He found her outside. She was lying on a mat at the back of the hut. There was an old woman by her side. The woman excused herself as soon as she saw him approach.

"Hey!" Adamma called out in a near inaudible voice, smiling as she raised her hand a little in offering. It seemed the scream had drained her of all her energy. He collected her hand as calmly and lovingly as possible. He couldn't believe his twin sister had ended up like this. He remembered all the poems she used to write. Whenever she wanted to tell him something of the gravest importance, she wrote it in a poem. Not the type that cracked your teeth like Christopher Okigbo but more like Niyi Osundare: something one could chew easily without the beauty being lost. Was this the same lady who looked at him now? He could see the pains in her eyes, even as a smile struggled to shove it aside. She was the most courageous being he had ever seen. How she ever agreed to keep the baby despite everything eternally puzzled him. She tried to talk but he urged her to be quiet. She persisted:

"I told them... I told them. That there was no need... to be kept inside... after all." She said weakly, even before he could say a word. *Had it been that long between the scream and now?* Then he noticed her blood soaked wrapper. Shock popped his eyes, waving lines to his forehead. Too weak to look down, she mentally followed his eyes to the wrapper. She said nothing.

"What happened?!"

She shuddered at the loudness of his voice which calmed his own shock. He reduced the tone of his voice. It was almost a whisper to match hers now: "What happened?"

Tears answered him. He placed her head on his laps and gently stroked her hair: *Was the baby dead?* Life sure had a way of changing things. He cursed himself for being the deep sleeper that he was. It didn't help matters that he had been drunk that night. It was perhaps, the reason she was here now. Had she forgiven him? *Would she ever forgive?* Memory relayed it all in a continuous present that refused to go past.

*

He wakes up in the middle of the sitting room, shocked. His surprise isn't at his being there. He doesn't usually sleep anywhere except in his room but he had gone out with friends to drink on the previous night. The taunts and all had got too much. There was no one around who would bother if he took a drink–or two. He was a man now and even if he wasn't, his parents had travelled out and wouldn't be back in a long while. Adamma, despite his love for her, wouldn't tell him not to. And he was going to be drinking palm wine which was not beer or alcohol in the real sense, right? He would take small, a single drink. He had reasoned in this light and stepped out. The single drink ended up in several calabashes of cool fermented palm wine. He somehow found his way home. He must have been too tired to go to the room...

Still, it is the way he wakes up that surprises him. He feels spent. It also seems that he has–had–been sexually excited someway. There are testimonies to this on his private part; his trouser button is loose and his penis is out. He looks around quickly to be sure that no one has seen him like this and adjusts his property properly as ought to be. It is then that he notices Adamma in a corner. She seems to be... No, she is sobbing. Had she seen him like that? He wonders. *He brushes his thoughts away and rushes to where she is:*

"Adamma, what is it?"

The question only brings a wail. What is wrong? *He does his best to comfort her but she pushes his hands and concerns away. He tries to get an answer from her without success for a long time. Later, she packs out to her friend, Dedoo's house. He keeps checking on her but she has already stopped talking to him. After his continued pressure and visits, she breaks the silence in a few words. She tells him that two men had claimed her maidenhood unjustly on the night he had got drunk. It seems strange to him that even as a listener to her tale, he feels it so strongly that he might have sworn that he had been there.* Maybe it is the work of an overactive imagination, *he thinks. There is something more but she will not say.*

Eventually, Dedoo tells him the full story as related by Adamma: The men had marched into the house with machetes. They did not take a single thing. They had barged into Adamma's room and dragged Adamma out to the sitting room and in a few minutes, took turns to rape her. During their forceful penetration, he had come in. The men seemed to be too busy to care. Adamma had called on him to rescue her. He simply stared on in his drunkenness. After a while, from obvious excitement, he zipped down and began to massage his penis. It didn't take him long to come. He smiled in satisfaction and fell to the ground, all spent...

Three days later, Adamma gets tired of Dedoo's one-bedroom apartment. Eating has become an issue. Then, there is the 'girl and girl as roommates' fracas that begins to emerge. As soon as their parents come back to town, Adamma moves back home. The story remains silent till a few months later when Adamma's stomach develops a bulge. The shocked parents wonder how this has come to be. On her part, she refrains from telling them the story. They consider disowning her but change their minds, parental feelings coming into check. There is a bargain though; she has to abort the child. No one is going to give birth to a bastard baby in the house of these church elders. Adamma refuses the offer. Not ones to be shamed, they put her in her rightful place, on the streets. After all, she isn't their only child. She stays with Dedoo for a while but issues come up once more. There is one option; the village. She takes it.

* *

He went to the old lady and asked what had happened. She was blunt and explained that Adamma had lost a lot of blood and they didn't believe she was going to make it.

"Her organs were not ready. The vagina was also too tight and we could have..." He didn't want to hear any more and shook his head vehemently to signify this. She shook her head in pity as the young man turned to leave.

He walked back to Adamma and saw her cradling the baby. The baby had been washed and brought to her. The child's dark skin contrasted with her milk brown skin. The strain of the task showed in the veins that shot out in her arms. It seemed Herculean but the smile on her face proclaimed the pride in her heart. It didn't hide the telling pain becoming evident. He knew she didn't have much time. Hatred rose in his heart for the 'little thing' in her arms. His fury also burned at the parents who had thrown their daughter out at a critical time as this. He had come to join her in the village after taking a long time to trace her whereabouts. He tried his best to do what sponsoring he could. She hardly spoke to him at all and he had counted it a miracle when she had smiled at him earlier on. His guilt always remained. He swore never to drink again but the pains of Adamma's sufferings kept getting to him... Maybe that was why he had found himself in the drinking hut that morning. He couldn't remember going there—

"Take care of my child for me," she said, bringing him to reality. She lay on the ground, the baby beside her. The pain was evident in her eyes. It looked as if she was using all her will power to stay alive. She looked at him with an expression he couldn't decipher, then, the stare became fixed.

"*Arrrrghhhrooooaaa!*" he howled, much like a wounded animal. He felt a deep ache in his head. He turned sharply as he heard sobs behind him. It was Dedoo. He looked at Adamma's face again. Though it had only been seconds, she seemed more peaceful now. He lifted his singlet to his eyes and mopped the free flowing tears. He turned to the baby who had taken his sister's life. The spite was evident in his eyes. Dedoo was wailing now...

* * *

It felt like thirty years though it was only a few days later. Time had lost its wings and crawled like a snail with twenty shells.

How can I take care of the child of a useless robber? He wondered on and on, punctuating the grief he continually expressed at his sister's loss. *It doesn't matter. I will simply end it all.*

He made a decision to kill the bastard who had taken his half away. He went to the hut where Dedoo was putting up. She went out to get something. In that little time, he mixed some lethal powder in water and tried to put it to the baby's lips. The baby looked into his eyes and a smile formed at its lips. He shuddered as he looked at the baby closely. Even at this stage, one couldn't miss how much it looked like him; the power of blood. *Maybe this is my new twin.* He shook his head. He wondered how he could think that after what the baby had done. At that moment, Dedoo stepped back inside. He handed the baby over to her:

"I am leaving back to the city to tell our parents what they have done."

"We can go together in two days' time *na*. Why don't you wait?"

"I want to get to them as soon as possible and let them know what has happened. Perhaps they will be happy now."

Dedoo did not particularly want to travel with him and so, didn't argue further. She stretched a note to him:

"What is this?"

"She told me to give it to you in case anything happened."

He opened it. The message was in lines—a poem. It was just like the Adamma of old. It had to be grave, whatever it was. Questions crowded his mind already; questions to throw at her. How convenient of her to keep it till now... The poem was titled 'One man.' It spoke of one man, never there being two to claim her prize. The man came in drunk and took that which tradition refused kin. A fool making half and half bring one as one left for the others to live. There was a P.S which was not so poetic. It simply made him know who the man was.

It made sense then sent him senseless.

ONE MAN
There were never two men
to claim my prize
One man

Drunken steps led to the sin
of one who took that which tradition
refused kin
A fool

Making the half and half
bring one full
As one leaves
that the others should live

HUNTING PIPES

E fe's forehead creased into knots in determination as if he was afraid that a little freer, he would lose his resolve. He looked around at his thatched hut. It was leaking in several places and made swimming, now impossible in the rivers, compulsory over here in every rain. The water could not be collected because of the chemicals mixed with it before its dropping—*black rains,* as the villagers came to know it. The land was polluted and was as infertile as the word 'barren'. Crops no longer grew, afraid of what would happen if they sprouted out. Preferring in, they died within the soil. They lay buried, like humans. Money was needed to resolve issues and get food that his people once sold! But where was the money? Ailments were on the rise and the level of illiteracy was increasing everywhere. He thought of all the hype created by the media paid for by the exploiting oil companies. The pictures were impressive. Efe kept marvelling at the ones in a magazine thinking what luck the people possessing them must have. A literate friend had gently tapped him and explained that the pictures were of the village they were in, his village! That evening, he had taken a tour of the village again, to be sure. Sure, the pictures didn't match.

Efe thought of the several explosions at the pipes and wondered if it was worth it. His elder brother, an empty coffin representing his missing parts, came to mind. He quickly shook his head, willing the memory away. He adjusted his shorts which sat loosely on his waist. He tied the rope as it squeezed around the material on his waist. Life was a risk; one had to take it.

He stepped out of his hut and into the compound. He was determined to look for any means possible to survive the times. His eyes fell on his siblings, three of them, sprawled on the bare floor. They looked on, pinching hunger describing the lines of the ribs that showed on their every feature. Rags for clothes, they looked to him.

"*Gud mo'rin broda,*" they managed to greet, as custom demanded, through parched lips. He did not know what to reply. He couldn't ask if they had slept well. He couldn't ask after their school, or if they were fine. The answers had been heard a million times over differently and were better left unasked. He hurried on, to hide the tears forming in his eyes. He walked on to his mother's door, passing his father and brother's graves. Her hoarse cough nearly hit him, as he came into the room. It seemed like her salutation to him. He stood by the door and replied,

"Mama, have you woken up? How is your health?" Still, questions not to be asked but compulsorily stamped in tradition. She stared blankly at him, seemingly asking how obvious things could be. Her health?

"Ef..." she started but was seized by a worse coughing session this time: *Kpof!! kpof!! kpohoof!!* He rushed to comfort her. He looked into her face. He noticed, not for the first time, the wrinkles occasioned by sufferings and ailments that had transformed her thirty-something year old face and body into a horrid eighty-ish caricature that hid tales of a one-time belle. She coughed again as a strange sound accompanied this time. A horrid smell came to his nose and he knew she had eased herself, unintentionally, right there. She had to see a doctor right away. He had had enough. He cleaned her up.

The lines on Efe's forehead were set in his resolution. He took some gallons from behind the house, his only inheritance. He grabbed his younger brother from the ground. He sought and joined some boys on their way 'pipe hunting'. As they walked, talk and laughter accompanied their pace. They soon found their quarry; there were other people there too.

"Why use the word 'hunt' when we simply walked to this area?" Efe asked. The others laughed at his inquisitiveness as they scooped oil from the broken pipe. He bent down to work soon forgetting his brother.

"It was left by some government people." Someone said without being asked any question. No one cared as they struggled for the 'crumbs,' filling their gallons.

No one noticed the little boy playing with sticks and two sharp stones hitting them—causing sparks.

When the media carried it the next day, they spoke in different words of Area Boys who for selfish ambitions sabotaged some oil pipes. Others spoke of the need for Government to do something to prevent such accidents. Somewhere, a mother looked through her door at two daughters, slowly dying to meet four males. She coughed, shaking fiercely in her excrement. It was only a matter of time.

WHAT WOULD BE

Tordoo was the baddest guy you could find anywhere. He was that in reputation anyway. He was a compendium of all the prettiest girls around. He was the marvel of the ladies and the envy—scratch that—vexation of the guys. A casual statistic of any fine lady would find that one in his so-called conquered trove. But even for the greatest of men, there is the lady to whom they will bow. For Tordoo, it was Nkiru. Not one of the 'fliest' or 'coolest' sounding names you could find even in the Igbo vocabulary but what did names have to do with anything? She had eyes that could hold you spellbound for years, just drinking of their depths. Call it ironic but she had a nose almost always running but one you would wish to catch at every chance. Her lips were something you'd hope to own for good; one to drink of forever. Her entire personage was a vision that could keep a million souls dreaming for an eternity. The problem was, she was his best friend and you know how that works: You have the goods but you can't really claim them.

However, at some point, fortune played chance his way and he took it as a sign to deal his card.

*

It was a reading. The love poet, Hyginus Ekwuazi was the man to listen to. Despite his apathy for roads, the poet had finally decided to come to Makurdi. Tordoo found this the opportunity to let it out. The strings of friendship had played too long. It was time to up the tempo. For the fifteenth time since he heard the news, he alternated a call from Anselm Ngutsav to Su'eddie, the guys organising the event.

"Ah, are you sure he's coming?"

"Na wa o. I gave you my word na. You ordinarily don't show so much interest. Hmmm, what is not happening with these your plenty questions?"

"You no go know. Thanks man."

"Is there anything I should wink about?"

Tordoo smiled. He knew that if he lingered on the phone too long, the ever calculating Su'eddie just would get the idea. That guy was something else. He ended the call and set to the planning: the readings to set everything in order, a visit to the university zoo and then dinner or something at Steam Restaurant. Then he'd let it out. What could possibly go wrong? He called Nkiru to book her Saturday.

* *

Friday night. Tordoo never took real relationships for granted. He knew that whatever happened the next day would mark a big difference in his life. He went on his knees to seek the directions of the heavens.

"Oh merciful One, if it be your will, make all things to go right..." After some time he added "But please, show me what you desire... Preferably, in a dream. Amen."

He lay on his bed, the lights out, staring at a ceiling he could barely see. He loved Nkiru, his faculty had confirmed it. He knew that asking any girl out would change the stance of that relationship. No friendship could last an asking out, he thought to himself. The casual beauty to it would be replaced by the deeper thoughts...What if she said 'Yes' out of pity? But the drums of his heart were beating too loud. He had to dance to their rhythm or get them to go hyper. He crossed himself and somewhere in his thoughts, found out he was hearing a voice from heaven; loudly, clearly.... *Saying what?*

He opened his eyes. It was still dark but the hours of sleep, far from over for many, were okay for him. He got up to begin his day...

* * *

The reading was far better than he could have imagined. By the time Tordoo and Nkiru got to the venue, there were some forty people and they had to squeeze into seats the organisers brought in later. The maestro had read out his poems alongside a surprise visitor, Musa Idris Okpanachi. They read out poem after poem, as if in competition for who the best lover could be; Okpanachi in a near Arabian tone while Ekwuazi pronounced each word carefully, as if to emphasise their worth in a low calm voice. He was no performing poet but his words were worth their weight in verse. The highlight was their final poems; Okpanachi's 'Half a poem' and Ekwuazi's 'The best poem I ever wrote'. Tordoo bought all the collections on display from the authors. He had been so engrossed in it all that he didn't really pay attention to Nkiru. He only remembered his manners when he had their books autographed. As he saw her name scribbled by Ekwuazi, something ticked in his head. One look at both of them and the crazy poet winked. Tordoo felt emboldened and somehow cornered the bard aside. He quickly laid his fears. Perhaps, the man of age could dish out some goodies.

"Oh boy, I see your eyes," Ekwuazi began, "The twinkle wouldn't always shine in your eyes. If it is you like that girl, let her know. We are all born with someone for us. Now, that person might be younger or older. Might be from your tribe or not. May be, she will be from another religion. At any rate, the truth is—and this is the point—if you let her go, you would always search for her in every other woman...for the rest of your life. The only excuse that can be condoned is if there is a case of madness in her family. Remember, if she is the one and you let her go, you will search for her everywhere, all your days."

Tordoo smiled and thanked him. He hugged the old man whom it came to as a shock:

"For luck," Tordoo added and rushed off to catch Nkiru who was getting tired of waiting.

"What was that about?"

"I just had to find some love tips from the guru."

"Who will you use that one on? Baddest guy! You don't need any love tip. Aren't you the encyclopaedia of feminine *over-sabi* and all?" She chuckled as she ended this but the joke seemed to escape him. "Okay, okay. Sorry. What's next?"

"To make up, I shall take you to the zoo. I guess you will meet your type there."

"What?"

"Hee hee hee! Lovely peacocks..."

"And your dear brother chimpanzee. Did I ever tell you that you look like a chimpanzee?"

Tordoo didn't take this kindly. Did she really think he was that ugly? Was there hope if she took him for that? She read his features in the worried quiz:

"Ah! Sorry o! Tordoo, what is so wrong with you today? You seem so uptight."

He eased up a bit and led the way to the zoo. There weren't too many animals there but it was fun to see nature. They walked towards the beach but she stopped at some point. She was aquaphobic. He laughed and she felt slighted. As Tordoo apologized, he wondered if the signs weren't obvious. He tried to remember his dream once more. The words hadn't been clear. It probably was a positive response. By the way, Ekwuazi had told him to go on. And that was exactly what he intended to do. There was one last place to get to: the orchestra playing at the IBB square. Just his luck, one didn't always find these things in Makurdi.

They had a most splendid time. The music was out of the world. At some point, Tordoo took her hands and led her to the dance floor. The beats were different from the regular mad rhythms demanding gyrating that typical Nigeriana afforded. This one teased the very centre of the soul. Slowly, the music caressed their souls and in each other's arms, they forgot the world. Somewhere between, he knew it was the time to ask. He looked into her face but her eyes were closed. He opened his mouth to whisper into her ears:

"Nkiru..."

"Yes..." It was a voice of expectation. He felt his spirit lift even as his heart emitted big booms that ran completely opposite to the slow tunes. She was now against his chest; her hair in his nose. He inhaled deeply the sweetness of the fragrance of her hair. He knew that nothing else mattered. He could spend the rest of his life here. Suddenly he understood what Peter had felt at the transfiguration:

"Nkiru, can we..." then he remembered the exact words of his dream. The voice had said: "Nkiru is not meant to be your wife." He closed his eyes as the tears rolled slowly. He knew he had to let her go. If she wasn't going to be his wife, there was no need to ask for any less. He couldn't lose her friendship. He remembered some hugs in the past that had eased him of several stresses. He smiled and blinked away the tears. He opened his eyes slowly and discovered she was looking into his face. The music was no longer playing and the other couples had vacated the floor.

"Yes? Tordoo, is everything alright? Did I do something wrong? What did I say?"

"No... Not... Nothin..." the tears choked him. She drew his head down, hugged him tighter and continued the waltz. They didn't need the music; it flowed from within them.

"I have something to tell you, Tordoo," she whispered.

"Yes?"

"Tersoo asked me out. What do you think I should say to him?"

Tersoo was a mutual friend of theirs. Tordoo's booms banged faster now. He looked at Nkiru; it was now or never. It was all or not at all. Her getting with anyone else would remove something from their friendship. She would be someone else's. But the dream remained... He thought of the direction of his dreams and wondered whether to defy them. *It takes a man to change his stars no matter the word of any force.* He looked up to the skies:

"Look at them, aren't they beautiful?"

Her eyes followed his gaze; there was a carpet of stars above.

"They are," she managed to say after a while, lost in the dazzle of the heavens.

"I will always have your back."

"What?" She stared into his face. He stopped the spinning and stepping. He took her hand and slowly pointed out individual stars like he had done many times before. It felt more intimate now and he had a feeling it was the first of many more or the last time. Star by star, he named them all, alongside constellations and added tales to a few: the rosary of the skies, Capricorn, Nova formations, Greek tales and his favourite stars—Orion's belt, the three wise men. As he brought his head down after the talk, it looked straight into hers and the stars seemed to twinkle in her orbs. He held his breath, amazed...

Then, she kissed him...

AWAITING

Oche had been in this position before, was a very confident man and was therefore prepared. He had faced several similar circumstances so though this was new in its own right, he remained calm. *Maybe it is only normal to feel this way,* he thought. He looked at the three men beside him in the waiting room. They were sweating profusely despite the heavy air conditioning. Okay, so he was different. He wondered why they were so tense. The final hearing in any case was inevitable. It was either you were discharged and acquitted or convicted. So, what was the fuss? Anyway, they were first timers so he could understand with them. With two girls behind, he was already a pro in the league. He smiled as he engaged them in conversation and lightened the atmosphere. The tension reduced considerably but he could still notice the sweat. And to think that it was said men never cared or felt ruffled. The doctor entered the room as all the men rushed *"Na my own!"* Each one said claiming the smile on the doctor's face for his personal good news.

"Mr. Bemsen Akighir!" The roundish young man ran forward smiling, tears in his eyes: "Bouncing baby boy!"

"Jesus! Aôndo!" Bemsen shouted as he hugged everyone around. He started telling jokes and Oche had to wonder if this was the same man who had looked so sullen a few minutes ago. He danced around and then, remembering something, turned to the doctor who he had forgotten in his ecstasy; "My wife, how is she?"

"She is very fine, Sir. She is sleeping and so is the baby."

Without another word, Bemsen rushed to go and see his angels. "But Mr. Akighir! Mr. Aki..." but the energetic young man was long gone in the direction of the ward. After a while, he came back, confusion on his face:

"Where are they?"

"I was about to tell you where they were when you ran out," the doctor said as he laughed and led Bemsen to his wife and child.

Oche smiled. Then, the waiting started all over again. He looked at his watch. The time was two in the afternoon. He had been here six hours already. He turned to two of the three other remaining men who shivered. "Calm down, my brothers." He tried to ease them. They looked at him from their seat as he smiled reassuringly at them.

"Thank you." They muttered in turns, stretching a bit to reduce their continuing worry. One of the other two men who were a little less disturbed stole the interest of the men talking on literature and politics. *Why was the doctor taking so long?* Three hours had now passed since they saw him last. Then, he entered with that beacon on his face.

"Na my own!" "It is mine!" The four men each shouted as they rushed to the doctor.

"Mr. Mas Udibago." The tall bespectacled man who had been entertaining stepped forward.

"Yes! *Sebi*, I told you people." He shook the three other men confidently as he accepted their congratulations and followed the doctor to see his people. A few minutes later, the doctor came again and took two men with him. Oche sat there watching as slowly water began to form pools on his body. What was happening? He looked at the remaining man beside him, questions in his eyes. The high rate of maternal deaths and infant mortality was something that no one could overlook. Most of the hospitals needed upgrading with staff getting better training. He had always wondered why this issue was on the Millennium Development Goals list. *The money can be diverted to something more worthwhile*, he had always argued.

"Even in those days before the white man, the rate had been low. With all the hospitals now, there is no need for such," he would be heard saying often to anyone who cared to listen. However, as he waited for his wife, his stance changed. It was seven o'clock when he stepped out to visit the toilet.

Oche came back to meet the room empty. The sweating became intense accompanied by a tension that he had never thought possible. The praying started without any deliberate effort. All the prayers and special devotions that had long been flushed in a part of his memory came flooding in torrents. Though two nurses came at different times to encourage him, he kept wondering what was happening within. He asked every person who wore a uniform. The latest person he asked, a security officer, looked at him confused. The officer tried to calm him for a while before disappearing. He said his Divine Mercy prayers which he had hitherto totally lost faith in. His eyes were wide and bloodshot. Then, by eight-thirty, as his watch proclaimed, the Doctor came in. Oche heaved a sigh of relief as he rushed to him.

"Doctor..." The word held the suspense that enveloped him.

"We tried our best, Sir—"

"No!" Oche shouted, his world going dark and crashing all around him.

"Cool it, Sir. We tried at normal delivery but your wife is going to need a CS. We want you to sign some papers and we will also need some blood." Oche speedily signed the forms. His blood didn't match his wife's. He quickly gave a nurse who had come in, some money for the blood to be bought from the blood bank for the transfusion. It had gone worse than he had ever imagined. Oche cried as his whole being came into his mouth. He remembered how he had often argued with his wife on the sex of the baby. She had said girl number three. *Opposed!* was the reflex answer that always came from him. To enforce his position he had gone shopping for the boy's clothes. His wife had gone ahead to buy girl clothes...

"God! Oh God!" He cried to himself and in his tears, a little slumber came. A hand tapped him as he jumped up. It was a doctor, a different one.

"We could not operate on your wife again." The tension started mounting again as Oche opened his mouth to scream. Then, he noticed the smile on the doctor's face: "She delivered naturally, a beautiful baby boy." Oche stood speechless as he looked at the doctor in shock. The tears became of warmth and happiness as he shook the doctor's hand vehemently. "Please, Sir, I still need my hand if I am to continue in this profession."

"Oh, I am so sorry." Oche said as he smiled his thanks. God! God! God! He opened his mouth to ask the doctor if he could see them when the doctor's beeper came on.

"Sorry, Sir. Emergency." He rushed off.

"But...but... but..."

A nurse rushed to Oche after a while and explained a strange story. The wife of the last man who had been with Oche was having a shortage of blood. Unfortunately, her husband's blood did not match hers too and to make matters worse, the blood bank was empty. She concluded that the blood he had earlier purchased was the only remedy to the pregnant woman's life. Oche was irritated that they were wasting so much time. He gave his permission for the blood to be used.

It is little wonder there is a high level of maternal deaths. What if he had been absent? That might have spelt another mother and child. He shuddered at the thought as he imagined the several mothers and might-have-been mothers who had lost their lives to such negligence and absence. So many children too! His mind went to the MDG item again and mentally noted that he ought to get involved as soon as possible. The operation proved successful as the woman was successfully delivered, too. The nurse led her husband to the waiting room. He knelt before Oche:

"God bless you, Sir. This is your child, Sir. His name is yours. God bless you!"

Oche answered and charged him to be a bit quiet. Soon the doctor came in for the last time to take the two men to their respective loves. It was just then that Oche remembered that he hadn't called to find out how his children at home were doing. Anything might have happened to them. And yes, how could he have forgotten how hungry he was? He yawned as he moved forward, and fell.

THE GAPING VOID

A cry heralds dawn: a cockcrow; a child's cry.

The fourth succeeding cry of this child brought chills. The father entered a little while later. He smiled at his wife and she tried to return it but the strain shouted silently in the pulling lines of her eyes.

"It is a boy," the local midwife said mirthlessly. "Another *ogbanje*."

Ogbanje. Did she have to rub it in? Didn't his shelled joy tell the tale perfectly?

But she wasn't finished: "Ogbanjes die but we shall do our bit first. We shall name him."

Anger flashed in his eyes. She had expected it. Several years but Ebuka just wouldn't learn. He could be trusted to believe in faith rather than ideal fate. He viewed custom as simply a course to which people willed that which will befall them. She wasn't surprised to see the anger that easily blazed through his eyes when he was unpleasantly taken by surprise, as now.

"He shall live!"

"Ebuka, it is customary that we name him since he is the fourth. We shall name him Ozoemena—*may it not happen again*. Don't bother, it is only for a few days and the name wouldn't matter anymore. Not to him. It will never happen again. So, take those eyes of coal and fry something else! We shall scar him now."

"Will the scarring prevent him from dying or coming back?"

He had proven it again: he knew nothing of tradition. He would think of the name as defeatist. She looked up at him. There was a deep sadness swimming in the waters of his eyes. It was twin of the anguish of a mother who had lost three sons few days after birth. Somewhere there lay hope. She pitied the couple. She was suddenly filled with anger at the wicked baby that was tormenting her brother and Adaora, his wife once more. With certain earnestness, she made two marks on either side of the baby's face. Hopefully, his tribe in the other world would reject him as a result of the scars. The ogbanje tribe never accepted a scarred one and thus, this child would not return. If he returned, they would know him by his marks. But may the heavens forbid!

"He shall live! For two years, he shall be your Ozoemena. After that, he shall be Victor."

Victor, she thought. She said a silent prayer that the boy would bear that name. She hoped but knew the sad truth Ebuka and his wife's blind faith was stopping them from seeing: ogbanjes die.

The baby started convulsing. The sun was up.

*

Ogbanjes die
They will delight you with a cry
Then, in early childhood die
Locate your tear bank, prepare your cry
They might deceive you a few years but by and by
Ogbanjes die...

* *

The women took the baby from the tired mother. Nkem, the midwife led them. The mother, Adaora was drained of all energy. Though she couldn't struggle with them, the tears in her eyes spoke her concern.

"We would scar the baby. Don't worry. She has suffered you enough," Nkem said. Adaora tried to hold them back at this point but the words failed. The tears rushed in torrents. Maybe they were right. But what if they weren't? Where was her husband? If he was around, things *would* have been different. Well, what could she do? She discovered that Nkem was still talking:

"...the baby is already weak. It has refused to eat to punish you. This wicked child; the scars would make your clan in the other world to reject you! You would die but you would never come back!"

Adaora turned her face away. It had been a full year, yet the baby had still decided to leave. *Oh*!

The baby made a weak cry. Does a cry herald dusk?

* * *

Victor was out of breath when he got to the house. His brownish white shorts were proof of where he was coming from—the street soccer pitch. He rushed into the kitchen, got his food and had it going down his throat at a rate that might have booked him a ticket if he was driving. He had grown into a strong boy with a stomach of endless depths. His parents had two more children after him; Nneka and Ozoemena-omalicha—a suspected *ogbanje*. The bond between Victor and Ozoemena-omalicha was strong but there were days when childhood joys made him nearly forget the existence of any other thing but his excitement, and stomach.

"Look at you," Nneka called out, coming into the sitting room where Victor sat eating, "Ozoemena-omalicha is dying in the room and all you can think of is your stomach."

The food turned into rough sand in his mouth. He shot into the room where Ozoemena-omalicha was. The baby lay on the bed, silent. Victor felt her heat as soon as he got into the room. Or was it just the room? In the dimly lit room, he could make out the marks on her face. Fresh wounds carved in the shape of lines. He wondered what they were. The little baby was shivering without a single sound.

He got to the bed and picked her up. She knew how to crawl. He placed her on the ground and she spread out straight like a stone. Something stung at his heart—a desperate alarm as if communicated by her.

He carried her and looked into her eyes. He saw deep in those wells of sight a slow departure. He hugged her and she clutched unto him like a magnet. Somehow, he felt it within—the receding waves of a river trying to come back. They were calling. He felt it. They were calling. Not even the marks would help. They were calling.

The burning figure clung to her brother like a rope, or that last straw. He confirmed it—she was leaving. His eyes burned and an anguish from deep within, the very floor of his soul, seeped through him. The hot tears poured freely, not enough as the cold claws of death seemed to come to snatch its prize, slowly, almost muttering the terrible words:

Ogbanjes die.

Adaora could almost hear it too. She struggled from her bed to the room. The picture of the *ogbanje* children rooted her to the doorway. The tears of her heart sealed the door of her mouth. Victor looked to her and the words choked out from her:

"Your sister has decided to leave us. There's nothing we can do."

They felt a cold coming closer. She couldn't bear it. She turned to leave and heard a whisper of Victor's voice:

"*Victor.*"

With failing strength, a mother's warmth joined burning tears to start a fight against the cold scythed one...

* * * *

She would forever wonder what sealed the chasm of the void...

Ogbanjes die.
Ogbanjes die when we don't let them live.

* * * * *

A cock crowed in the distance. It was dusk.

DILEMMA

Boror looked at his drunken secretary. He knew he had to do something about her soon. He had come to this party with his wife and secretary—and had planned to be very brief but...that was the thing with women. *You could never really be brief especially if they were having a nice time which translated to enough to talk about with an acquaintance or the other*, he thought to himself bitterly.

He had met many old friends and, of course, colleagues were in their numbers here as it was a party that had been organized by the company. The music was sobering, and the lights seemed to have some magic on them. They were mild, coming from bulbs in the ceiling set at different angles. Soft music flowed in from hidden speakers. Boror decided it wasn't a bad idea to have spent some more time. He was quickly warming to it, mentally thanking his wife who had insisted that they should stay a bit long, when he noticed his secretary. She was getting too comfortable with the men around. He didn't need any gift to prophecy she might well be on her way to losing her job soon—from the bosses or with pressure from their wives. Really, which wife would like to see the huge bosom of another lady rubbing off on her husband? She was with Oga Adebola, the General Manager. Boror looked at Mrs. Adebola's face which seemed to be burning with enough coals for a full grill. Those eyes! Ah! With those eyes! Tonia! Tonia. *Kai.*

Tonia wasn't just any secretary. Boror had come a long way with her personally and professionally. He knew what it would cost him if she lost the job. Starting all over again, getting a good secretary, training anew and building a good relationship. Most of all, the confidentiality! How could one measure that? It could well take a millennium. His wife even agreed with her. Okay, then there was the fact that he would have another dependant—Tonia had no one else but him. No! He had to grab her from the shackles of termination. Come to think of it, he was the one who had brought her here and thus, was responsible for her.

Snap out of it! One part of him seemed to say. *She is a big girl and should be responsible for her actions. After all, it seems being drunk is a part of her.* Yeah, but she was no drunk. He knew that she was probably under stress and had decided to cool it off much to the detriment of the bottles. Boror began to wonder why it was characteristic of people to throw themselves at alcohol once they were stressed. That always seemed to elude him for as he loved to put it, *they clear your head a bit and later on bring a heavy heartedness once clear headedness is restored.* Wasn't it also funny that once ladies fell under the wondrous spell of the bottle, they made themselves vulnerable?

With a start, he discovered that he had been unconsciously trying to prolong his thoughts in order to forget his secretary's state. He approached her group and excused her. He took her to his car and ignited the drive to her house. He looked at her and noticed she was already sleeping—and noisily too.

So young women snore? He smiled to himself.

Screeeeeeeeeeech!

That was close, Boror thought to himself as he looked through the window at the boy he had nearly crushed. Unlike the usual motorist, no word came to his mind for the boy and as such, he continued his journey. The boy was amazed and wondered if at that instant he had been teleported to a different country. No insults? He had expected Boror to probably park and give him a thrashing—that is if he had caught him. He was disappointed.

Screeeeeeeeeeech!

The smell of burning rubber. He was still on the road and this time knew he was not going unpunished. The boy took to his heels amid several insults from the recent motorist.

Boror thought about the boy. He looked at Tonia and imagined a drunken mother not caring about her son's location. He was already at the house and helped her out of the car. He asked her for the keys and she handed him her handbag. Interesting, he thought to himself, she was drunker than he had thought. How he knew? For heaven's sake, which other lady would hand you her bag like that? He searched her bag and found the keys. He opened the door and led her to her bed. He noticed that her shirt was rather too tight and had been giving her breathing problems.

No wonder the snore.

Srrrrrap!

Without thinking, he *had* briefly helped her get rid of it. The quite young, rich and ample chest heaving up and down was the only thing that told him of what he had just done. He quickly took his hands off her. He took a glance at her upper half...

Quite beautiful.

He looked at her face; a warm comforting smile played at her lips. Or was it inviting? He sure had a beautiful friend. Several ideas fleetingly crossed his mind. She looked quite humble now and so...

Oh no!

He had left his wife at the party. He looked at his watch, it was eleven o'clock and she had spoken of them leaving at that time so as to get something at a super eatery. He raced quickly and as he drove, he scanned the car to check if any of his secretary's things had been left to give a wrong impression. He remembered an advertisement for a fast car that he had watched. A man had taken his lady to an airport and noticed that she had forgotten her makeup. Quick as flash, Mr. Goodman raced and arrived just as the plane was reaching its destination. Smiling, he took the makeup kit like a prized possession. The knight handed it to his lady. "But hon," she began, "that isn't mine." And the rest, as the artists would put it, is best imagined. He laughed out loud at this memory. These people could give fantastic tales. And now, to be sure, he double checked. He could never be made that foolish, he thought, a smile still playing at his lips—obviously a relic of his earlier thought.

He arrived just in time—to find his wife looking for him and quite angrily too! That spelt TROUBLE in any dictionary, he could bet for a million naira any day. She marched straight to the car.

"Hey! Hey Love," he tried to compensate as he drew near for a kiss or peck? Whatever, none was coming forth. Wow. It seemed not even a box of chocolate and a bunch of roses would have worked.

She got into the car without a word. He drove on cruise speed and tried to brighten her up with what he hoped were jokes. No change. He decided to flatter her on her outfit; ladies love those things, you know? He looked at her to assess and see what attribute of hers he could innocently flatter. In that instant, he noticed the lone shoe. *Damn!* He thought he had looked properly before. How on earth was he going to get rid of it before his wife noticed? He decided to tell her where he had been and why he was late, he opened his mouth:

"Love..." he started but stopped mid track. Which mentally sound woman would believe that after taking a 'preference' for one's young beautiful secretary—who was drunk; laying her in bed and helping her 'feel free', nothing happened? He decided to distract her and get rid of the offending object:

"Well, you know Love, there seem to be a lot of new buildings about." She did not as much as bat an eyelid. Okay. "See how that church shines so brightly in the night." Still, no way. Maybe, "A skyscraper here!" No show. Several more tries; desperation.

Haba, why wasn't this woman cooperating or making things easier na?

"A new multipurpose salon and fashion centre?"

"Where?" she asked, quickly looking out to the right. Time enough as Boror briskly bent in a second and sent the naughty offender out the driver's window, mercifully into a gutter or was it a ditch? *Smiles.*

"I knew you would finally come around chic!" he said, elated at his twin successes. He put on the radio and hummed as they sped along to the expensive eatery, he usually avoided, much to his wife's joy and excitement. Or so he hoped. He was a happy man indeed. They reached their destination and his wife stepped out and started searching for something on the floor of the side of the car she had just vacated.

Oh no! Boror thought as panic seized him. Had she seen the shoe before he threw it? *No way, it wasn't possible.* He calmed himself down and asked; "Love, what are you looking for?"

"Honey, did you see," tension "one leg of my shoes?"

THE MIND OF TIME

They lit up like dandelions and were blown out when I told the time...like moons that fade with morning, like spent stars, cosmic seeds, dust-worlds, drifting into oblivion...
But the rest is never silence, sirs, it is loud with doubt and eloquent with the unsaid.
— Christopher Rush, *Will*

Demekpe got to the path that led to his house. There was no one about and he smiled in relief. He walked cautiously, a question in each raised step: *Why are people acting weird towards me? Why are they running away?* He might have joined them but where were they heading to? What was this recurring fainting that had become his portion? He was moving in many places and doing several things at once. *What really is this all about?*

Events had sprinted fast into a blur. His memory bank held no account of the last few hours. He hoped that the serenity of his house would guide him back to a sanity he felt ebbing away.

Demekpe pushed the gate open and felt panic rush at him like a wind. Where was his jeep? Maybe he hadn't driven it to the village. His younger brother and travelling companion, Chiven would know but where was Chiven? Ordinarily, Demekpe would have taken a tour of the grounds especially as he had not been here in some time but the weight of exhaustion squashed the thought of any such exercise. He stepped into his living room and headed for his favourite couch.

"I am tired," he said to no one in particular.

If this was the house in the city, he would have put on the TV to watch some Aljazeera. Here, he had ensured the absence of all those. It was his resting place. He closed his eyes but opened them almost as soon as he did. *What has happened here?* He thought. With the exception of his couch, the position of every other furniture had changed from the way he had left them. *Who was responsible?* Was it the boys out of their own stupid discretion? Was it Mngu, his wife? *Wouldn't these questions cease? Well, someone has to start giving answers now.*

"Tor! Tor! Tor!"

Silence answered his call. This was the thing about the village house. People hardly stayed around. Once he didn't tell them he was coming, they all went where they pleased, coming back late.

"Tor!"

It dawned on him that Tor was meant to be in school; his university was in session at the state capital.

Wait a minute. I am meant to be in the state capital actively involved in the case against that rogue of a political dictator imposed on us. They were in court over the last gubernatorial elections. Demekpe was one of the key plaintiffs fighting the case of the opposition. So, why was he elsewhere? What was going on now? Those results? He dug into his trouser pockets and searched right up to the thread that lined them. He turned his pockets out; they were empty. Where were his phones and wallet? The hooks of the question marks were getting too many. He just had to remember something...anything! *Well, isn't it only appropriate that the house should be empty? Maybe I should just enjoy the silence and rest.*

At that moment, Tor came in. Demekpe looked up, eyes wide:

"Aren't you meant to be in school?"

The boy stiffened, his entire features frozen as if he were a statue pushed into the house by someone else. Demekpe wondered at the Medusa effect.

"Are you not the one I asked a question?" No response. On a different day, he might have *blessed* the boy with a slap to shake him out of rigidity. For now, he felt dizzy and decided to ignore Tor's play. "Get me some water to bathe. Now!"

That seemed to thaw Tor out of his frost. His mouth hung open and though he made some movement, he stayed fixed to the spot. Demekpe felt the blankness coming. He fought it a bit but found it consume him. Darkness descended: "I am tired..."

*

Demekpe woke up.

Where was he? His head ached. He looked around at his scattered living room. How had he come here? What happened? There were bloodstains on his shirt but he had no idea of this. He heard some sniffing from outside and stood up to find out who was crying. He headed out. His voice heralded his coming:

"*Ka ana la?*"

The crying person didn't seem to hear him. It was his nephew, Bunde, shivering away with two lines streaming down his face; mucus forming bubbles from his nose; and a chaplet in his hands. His head was slightly bent, his attention on the floor as his hands rolled each rosary bead, lips forming words not affected by his cry. He seemed to be in a drugged daze. It was strange to see him this way for Bunde was a sharp dresser whose comportment was always proper. Demekpe walked towards him slowly. The first question would have been to ask what the boy was doing in the village when he should have been busy at work in the city but fatherly concern seemed to overrule this time:

"Bunde."

"Dadi!!" Bunde looked up sharply, his deep red eyes bulging up in surprise. It seemed he had been crying long.

"Why are you crying?"

Demekpe had never liked softness in men and knew that Bunde was a strong man. Something must have gone horribly wrong for him to be in tears; he had not even cried at his own father's burial. Demekpe smiled at the young man in front of him. Who would have believed that this was the child his sister had brought to his house as a finger-sucking two-year old? Memories of a certain night many years ago played strongly in his mind. The entire household had sat in the living room watching *Things Fall Apart* on NTA. Bunde, as had come to be usual, had his finger stuck in his mouth. To dissuade him from sucking, they had tried wounding the finger; putting pepper on it, and all sorts of other things. The boy had always found a way out. He had washed the pepper off; sucked the wound painfully and finding no way to heal and enjoy the finger at the same time, switched fingers. They had tried several other things but the more they brought new tactics, the more Bunde triumphed. At first, Demekpe had beaten the boy to make him change. He had supervised the various methods used. The boy just would not stop! On that night, as they watched TV, he noted his eldest son trying to correct Bunde. Demekpe's eldest son had forced the finger out of his mouth. The boy had stubbornly put it back in. Everyone expected Demekpe to slap Bunde into obedience. After all, Bunde's arrogance was against discipline and all he—Demekpe—stood for. They all looked to see what Demekpe would do. That night, he could only smile at the courage of the small boy; the courage to stick to what he wanted at all times and defy all—even him. Demekpe did not like the sucking but he sure admired the boy's steadfastness.

"Leave my son," Demekpe had declared in a final ruling that left everyone in the living room shocked. He had found a permanent place in the boy's heart...

The grown Bunde hugged Demekpe tightly. Now, Demekpe was confused. Hadn't Bunde just been crying? Sure they had grown close but he never went too chummy with his children. Most affection ended in talks or slight side hugs. Laughs and other non-touches were the accepted limit. It always felt strange to get hugs. He was regarded as very strict and not emotional; one not to hug back. A handshake was usually a big sign of affection. The hug was welcoming, he had to admit. He hugged Bunde back briefly.

"Wan ikya!" It was his way of lightly teasing his children—small monkey. One of them had once replied him saying: "Daddy, yes, I am a small monkey but you are my father." That child's buttocks had paid dearly.

Bunde wiped his eyes and smiled in response:

"Dadi."

"Why were you crying?"

"Nothing...you...eh..."

He fixed Bunde a stare that carried the full import of his question:

"What is it?"

Demekpe noticed that there was still some puzzle in Bunde's eyes despite the glee that had come over him:

"What is it? Why are you looking like you have seen a ghost?" At this question, a small shadow came over Bunde's features. But he kept quiet, a smile still playing at his lips.

"Are you deaf?" No answer. "Bunde!"

That brought him back: "Dadi!"

"Am I talking to the wall or a human being?"

Silence again. What was it with everyone today? Demekpe noted that Bunde had an eyebrow arched up, his other eyelid somewhat lowered. His forehead was creased in waves and a studious frown replaced the previous silly smile that had seemed plastered on his face. It didn't look like Bunde was prepared to share what pressed his heart so Demekpe switched to a different question:

"What happened to everyone around? They all seem to be running from me. Do I have a mixture of chicken shit and leprosy on my body? Am I now a masquerade or ghost?"

Bunde giggled at this but seeing the stern look on Demekpe's face, coughed lightly:

"Dadi, you have...are...eh..."

"My friend, don't get me angry!!"

The children all knew that this was the sign that they had pushed him to the edge and exhausted his patience. The last kiss of his whip on their buttocks had been felt long ago but the memories stayed forever. More than that, Demekpe's anger had come to be respected for what it was—fiery. The risen tone always brought an answer.

The boy must be hiding something, Demekpe thought to himself. He decided to ask one last time, his hand gearing to support his mouth if an answer didn't come forth:

"I said—"

"Dadi, you are dead."

"What?"

"You are dead."

"You are crazy!" *Bunde has really gone mad. Sad. Sad. Sad.*

"Can you remember what happened to you...?"

Demekpe followed Bunde's pointed finger to the bloodstains on his shirt.

"You were shot, we were told." He pointed to a grave that Demekpe beheld; his.

"How?" *How can it be?*

"You don't remember?"

Demekpe bit his lips, and scratched his thick beards as he willed his mind to claw through the thicket of his acquired amnesia.

"We would never forgive all of them who did it! Never! I tried to imagine how you had passed on, with that smile..."

"I had a smile on?"

"Yes. And you were the only one who died—"

Demekpe smiled, "I, who died from shots, went on with smiles and you are crying?"

"But—"

"I am here and you are still holding to hurt?"

"But—"

"I still don't understand this..." Demekpe said. The wavy lines of his forehead showed his confusion. It started to come slowly; the memory of a drive... Then, it faded.

"Why am I here then?"

* *

He woke up.

Where was he? His head ached. He looked around at the scattered living room. How had he come here? What happened? He didn't seem to remember a thing of the immediate past. He needed a bath to clear his head and think. He heard some sniffing from outside and stood up to find out who was crying. He headed out. His voice heralded his coming.

A FINAL SHORT STORY TO SAY *Thank You...*

Our people say that a community can feed a man... can a man feed a community?

The journey to the final manuscript was filled with thorns and ugly thistles. The first editors, Tochi Nicole Brown and Tavershima Ayede had the right instruments to clear them. Su'eddie thanks them all, but had to apologize, being human, for whatever errors his blunt devices brought forth. Adewunmi Adeduntan did amazingly with 'Puzzles.' Regina Achie-Nege did the final cleaning.

Tales have their genesis somewhere: The verse of a certain lady, Gbubemi Pessu, titled 'The Music from the other room' inspired the short story of the same title. One evening the wondrous poet, Dr. Hyginus Ekwuazi, told Su'eddie a story of his life. Somehow, it formed the foundation for 'The Gaping Void'. 'A Tale of another's Crime' started as a dream and was written in dedication to Iember Nor. 'Smiles, Sighs and Groans' was written for a big sister, Mercy Njideka Adeduntan. That tale ('Smiles...') is dedicated to Dotta Raphels, Aturmercy, Dora Oyana, Dooyum Tsavsar, Hembadoon Itakpe and Sibbyl Whyte. Now, maybe a few other tales had their own stories too... Maybe.

Geoff Ryman gave some tips to the author—most which he hopes to apply in subsequent editions...

Okay, Mr. Writer, let me take over from here...

Chuma Nwokolo has been a great teacher and friend. Carlos Ruiz Zafon, Abubakar Adam Ibrahim and Reward Nsirim remain writers who inspire me. Elnathan John in many ways helped me to shape 'Puzzles' and gave me hope when I am sure he never knew. The critique sessions at Abuja Writers' Forum helped to make me far better. I am grateful to Dr. Emman Shehu for the forum and for his work on supporting literature. The Association of Nigerian Authors has also been a supportive body giving me a platform to launch several ideas. Thanks to Remi Raji, Denja Abdullahi, Maiwada, and the ANA top team for their work at the national level. Naija Stories and the Benue ANA group on Facebook gave me a platform to put up some of these tales. I got lots of encouragement and also constructive criticism from there. I really would have named most of the people there but that would be naming a galaxy of writers. Still, Myne Whitman, Kaycee Uzochukwu, Seun Odukoya,

Gboyega Otolorin, Lawal Opeyemi, Ife Watson, Enoquin, Gooseberry, Jefsaraurmax, Shanu 'Shai' Afolami, Thank you Myne Whitman for that platform. It means much. Ada Agada, thank you for your commitment to literature. Sometimes, you have issues but overall, well done on all you do. Thanks to Drs Maria Ajima and Andrew Aba for their support through time.

The SEVHAGE Editorial assistants, Debbie Iorliam and Sewe Leah Anyo have proven friends time and again. They gave me various tips on the work and asked certain questions that made me make the final selection that have become this work. Debbie has remained one fascinating lady that one cannot help but be grateful for. Thaddeus Naor, Terese Uwuave and Eugene Odogwu, thumbs up for the production we do. Jay and Nath Aduro, Jennifer Emelife, Sibbyl Whyte Onyeocha, Nkemjika Xtien Okeke, Ene Odaba and Anselm Ngutsav have been of help inspiring me to move on at different moments, thanks guys. My friends, Kukogho Iruesiri Samson, Femi Morgan, Dami Ajayi and Servio K. Gbadamosi: good work with promoting literature guys. Azafi Omoluabi *et Ra*: You raise the bar. Well done.

Regards are due Sam Ogabidu, a friend through the years, Tubal Rabbi Cain and Omadachi Oklobia, patrons whose help has eased some literary and developmental challenges. Mrs. Eugenia Abu has remained a mentor and I thank her for a lot words can't say. Johua Agbo, Maik Ortserga, Andrew Bula and Pever X are pals whom I have sipped several toasts that have inspired more critical thinking. I salute Myles Idoko Ojabo for being my brother and being the artiste that makes the role of the writer come alive each time. I am grateful to my paddies: Sonnen Gire, Alu Iperen, Victor Olugbemiro, Rosarii Gberikon, Yakori Mohammed, Sola Abisagbo, Teror and Solo Chen, Ololade Olatunji, Inalegwu Oklobia, Femi Adewunmi and Bunmi Olateju for so much. Ternenge Torough, Mlumun and Evelyn gave me board. Merci! Ugbor Ogochukwu has stood by me through much. Thank you, nwa nnem. Agatha Aduro has been far more than words can say; a heart's thrill, a soul's song any day. Thank you for being there. To my siblings, those to whom this collection is dedicated and others including Ngodoo, Ngohide, Terhide, Tersoo, Sefa, Fanen, Av and Verun: I am honoured to have you here. For all the wahala, thanks. The Shangos, Ayedes, the Adzeges (Fafa et Sewie mi), Agemas—Schola, Victor, Aver, Chinedu, Lolo...and all—una well done. To Chris Ayede-Agema: thanks for the love and every single support, you make it worth it.

And on the vast sheets of the subconscious, he wrote the names of the million others that the limitations of paper didn't help him praise. A little note was added as he let them know that they meant far more than a few scattered thanks on dozen leaves could say. They were in his prayers each day and he prayed that the times be truly kind for them all and everyone of us. Amen.

Su'eddie Vershima Agema is the author of Bring our casket home: Tales one shouldn't tell (longlisted for the Association of Nigerian Authors Poetry Prize 2013). His poem, 'Tales one shouldn't tell often' was shortlisted for the Saraba/PEN Nigeria Poetry Prize 2013. Su'eddie was included in EGC's Top 50 Nigerian Contemporary Poets in 2013. He is the Chairman of the Association of Nigerian Authors (Benue State Chapter), a member of the Abuja Writers' Forum, as well as Editor and Executive Officer at SEVHAGE Publishers. Su'eddie's personal blog is http://sueddie.wordpress.com. He also blogs at http://sevhagereviews.wordpress.com, http://naijastories.com/author/sueddie @sueddieagema on Twitter. He can be reached at eddieagema@yahoo.com.